1) Don't go to the family ranch while your fiancé is out of town and spend lots of time with his brother.

2) Don't listen to your heart pounding madly whenever your fiancé's brother is near.

3) Don't wish for a marriage based on true love—stick to one that your head tells you is right, even if your heart doesn't agree.

4) Don't compare the two men—you might find you like the brooding, arrogant black-sheep brother better!

Dear Reader,

This month, Silhouette Romance unveils our newest promotion, VIRGIN BRIDES. This series, which celebrates first love, will feature original titles by some of Romance's best-loved stars, starting with perennial favorite Diana Palmer. In *The Princess Bride,* a feisty debutante sets her marriage sights on a hard-bitten, cynical cowboy. At first King Marshall resists, but when he realizes he may lose this innocent beauty—forever—he finds himself doing the unthinkable: proposing.

Stranded together in a secluded cabin, single mom and marked woman Madison Delaney finds comfort—and love—in *In Care of the Sheriff,* this month's FABULOUS FATHERS title, as well as the first book of Susan Meier's new miniseries, TEXAS FAMILY TIES. Donna Clayton's miniseries MOTHER & CHILD also debuts with *The Stand-by Significant Other.* A workaholic businesswoman accepts her teenage daughter's challenge to "get a life," but she quickly discovers that safe—but irresistibly sexy—suitor Ryan Shane is playing havoc with her heart.

In Laura Anthony's compelling new title, *Bride of a Texas Trueblood,* Deannie Hollis would do *anything* to win back her family homestead—even marry the son of her enemy. In Elizabeth Harbison's sassy story, *Two Brothers and a Bride,* diner waitress Joleen Wheeler finds herself falling for the black-sheep brother of her soon-to-be fiancé.... Finally, Martha Shields tells a heartwarming tale about a woman's quest for a haven and the strong, silent rancher who shows her that *Home is Where Hank is.*

In April and May, look for VIRGIN BRIDES titles by Elizabeth August and Annette Broadrick. And enjoy each and every emotional, heartwarming story to be found in a Silhouette Romance.

Regards,

Joan Marlow Golan

Joan Marlow Golan
Senior Editor Silhouette Books

Please address questions and book requests to:
Silhouette Reader Service
U.S.: 3010 Walden Ave., P.O. Box 1325, Buffalo, NY 14269
Canadian: P.O. Box 609, Fort Erie, Ont. L2A 5X3

TWO BROTHERS AND A BRIDE

Elizabeth Harbison

Silhouette

R O M A N C E™

Published by Silhouette Books

America's Publisher of Contemporary Romance

Thanks to Cris Grace for the perfect editorial touch, and
to Mary Kay McComas, whose writing never fails to
inspire me.

SILHOUETTE BOOKS

ISBN 0-373-19286-X

TWO BROTHERS AND A BRIDE

Copyright © 1998 by Elizabeth Harbison

This edition published by arrangement with Harlequin Books S.A.

Printed in U.S.A.

Books by Elizabeth Harbison

Silhouette Romance

A Groom for Maggie #1239
Wife Without a Past #1258
Two Brothers and a Bride #1286

ELIZABETH HARBISON

first thought of becoming a writer in sixth grade, when she would stay up well past midnight reading Nancy Drew and Trixie Beldon books by flashlight under the covers. The idea became a decision when she discovered the books of Mary Stewart and Dorothy Eden, and realized that writing would be a really *fun* thing to do for a living.

She studied literature and art history at the University of Maryland and the University of London, Birbeck College. She's been back to England once since college and is eager to return again, and possibly even set a book there.

The author of several cookbooks, Elizabeth spends her spare time cooking, reading, walking and shopping for new books. As for romance, her fairy-tale dreams came true in 1994 when she married her real-life hero, John, a musician and illustrator. They currently reside in Germantown, Maryland, with their daughter, Mary Paige, and dog, Bailey.

Elizabeth loves to hear from her readers. You can write to her at P.O. Box 1636, Germantown, MD 20875-1636.

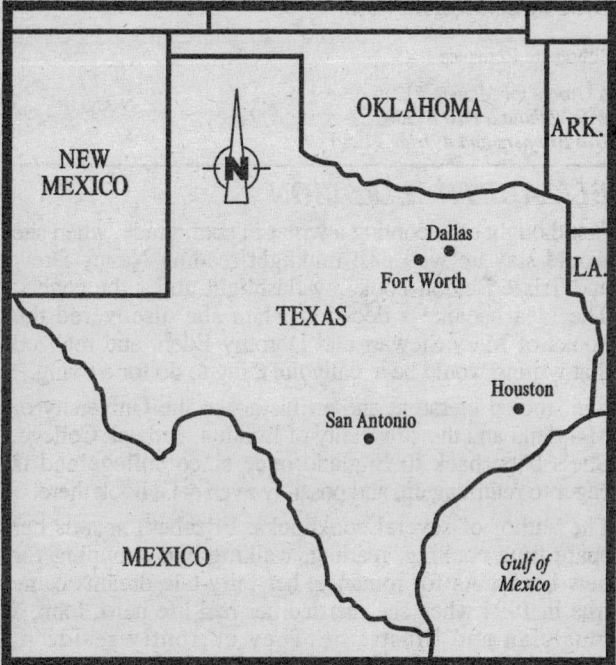

Chapter One

"Twenty-nine years in this tiny town—"

"Thirty. I turned *thirty* last month."

"Okay, thirty years. But you're finally gettin' out of here, Joleen. Honey, life's turnin' good. This is what your mama always wanted for you, and I'm so happy I could burst. Marrying Carl Landon! Child, you'll never have to work again!"

Joleen Wheeler wiped a tear from her cheek with the back of her hand. "Marge, I didn't say I'd marry him." For some reason she clung to that thought like a life raft. "In fact, I'm not even sure going with him to Dallas for so long is such a great idea." She pressed her lips together and shook her head. She knew Marge and all the other girls at the Hometown Diner thought she was nuts to even hesitate leaving this steaming, greasy pit that smelled so strongly of hamburger and onion that she had to shower to get the scent off her at night.

Marge put her hands on Joleen's shoulders and pressed her weathered face toward her. The familiar scent of onion mingling with Marge's old-fashioned Yardley lavender perfume nearly brought tears to Joleen's eyes.

"Jo, honey, you listen to me," Marge said vehemently. "When your mama died, her last wish was that you wouldn't stay working in this no-count diner in this no-count little town for the rest of your life." She'd always wanted to stop waiting tables, but she'd died before she had the chance. Marge's watery blue eyes were more impassioned than Joleen had ever seen them. "People get stuck here in Alvira and they never get out. This is the opportunity of a lifetime. Don't miss it 'cause of some grand notion about bein' in love."

Joleen gave a wry laugh and touched her finger to the wrinkled cheek of her mother's oldest friend. "Marge, I don't think loving the man you marry is a *grand notion*."

Marge snorted and raised her chin, somehow managing to look down her nose at Joleen, who was a good five inches taller. "It is when it's stopping you from marryin' an oil tycoon."

Joleen pulled back and walked to the corner jukebox. "I didn't say I *wasn't* going to marry him, either. I only said I wanted a little bit more time to be sure...to be sure it *is* love and not something else." *Desperation*, she thought, then pushed the thought away.

"Whatever it is, it's worth marryin'."

"We'll see." Joleen reached into her pocket for a

quarter and pulled out instead the huge diamond and
sapphire ring Carl had given her as a "token of his
affection." She looked at the ring for a moment, then
sighed and put it back. "But, you know, his insisting
that I move to his family's ranch in Dallas for the
summer so I can 'see how good it feels to be a Landon' makes me a little uncomfortable." Unable to
find a quarter, she pressed B3 and gave the machine
a well-placed kick. Patsy Cline's "Crazy" started
playing.

"How can you be uncomfortable about living in
a big ol' house with air-conditioning for the summer?" Marge asked incredulously.

"It's not the air-conditioning I'm uncomfortable
with, God knows." Jo lifted her pale hair off the
back of her neck and let it fall with a heavy flop.
"It's the 'being a Landon' part. I'm not sure I can
do it if they're so different from the rest of us."

"Honey, it's just the *surroundings* that are different," Marge said. "The Landons eat, drink and go
to the bathroom like the rest of us."

Joleen laughed. "I'm not even sure about *that.*"

Marge shrugged. "Well, if they have one of those
bidet things, you'll learn to use it like the queen."

"I think it's pronounced be—*day,*" Joleen said,
then reconsidered. "But I'm not sure. Oh, good Lord,
Marge, what if it overflows and I have to tell someone and I call it the wrong thing?"

"Now, Joleen, don't borrow trouble. You're going
to do just fine."

"I sure do wish I shared your confidence."

Marge regarded her in silence for a few minutes,

then said, "Child, you can do anything you set your mind and heart to do."

Joleen wasn't quite sure what Marge meant by that, but before she could ask, the small bells over the diner door tinkled. They both turned to face it, Joleen automatically smoothing her denim skirt where her apron would normally have been.

A tall man, about mid-thirties, with dark brown hair and light eyes walked in, looking a little like a lost tourist. As soon as she saw him, Jo couldn't look away.

He wore faded jeans that fitted him in a way that would have brought tears of joy to Levi Strauss's eyes. His plain white cotton shirt was clearly high quality even though he wore it as casually as if it were an old T-shirt, with the sleeves rolled up. Joleen couldn't help but notice the way it pulled slightly at the shoulders, suggesting a powerful physique beneath. His arms and the triangle of skin at his neck where the top button was undone were a deep sun bronze.

Even the laugh lines carved into his tanned face, next to those pale eyes and that sensually curved mouth, added to his magnetism. A woman would have hated to have those lines herself, but on a man they were like trophies, well earned and a pleasure to behold.

Joleen realized she'd sucked in her breath and let it out slowly. She felt like a high school girl gawking at the football captain. All her fears about marriage, which she had worked so hard to ignore, spilled into her mind. This was just the sort of man fate would send her way when she was trying to convince herself she could fall in love with Carl and stay with him for the rest of her life. A western Adonis, a Marlboro man without the cigarettes.

He had to be a mirage.

He glanced at the door behind him then back at Marge, and then Joleen.

There his eyes lingered, holding Joleen's gaze as easily as a carnival hypnotist. The seconds stretched on, past the point where casual interest left off and *Howdy stranger, want to come to my place?* picked up. Except that Joleen wasn't that sort of girl. Normally.

Now, for just a moment, she was able to imagine being that sort of girl... Until her logical mind snapped her out of it. This wasn't fate, this wasn't love at first sight, this was a normal, if extreme, reaction to a fear of commitment. It could have been Hank the barber coming in and she would have had the same second thoughts about Carl. Well, maybe not the *exact* same thoughts, but second thoughts nevertheless.

It was Marge who broke the awkward silence. "Stayin' for the early bird special tonight?"

His eyes moved over to Marge. Joleen felt like a rag doll dropping to the floor, no longer suspended by his gaze.

"I'm looking for Julie Wheeler," he said in a smooth masculine voice. But the end of his statement turned up like a question and he looked back at Joleen.

"Jo—" Joleen began, but Marge nudged her with her elbow.

"And just what do you want with this Julie Wheeler?" Marge asked, crossing her arms in front of her. Marge was used to deflecting suitors and creditors alike.

One of the man's eyebrows lifted fractionally, as if he sensed that and was amused by it. "I want to take her home with me." The corners of his compelling mouth remained suspiciously tight, and Joleen was tempted to laugh except that her heart was in her throat.

She knew this man, somewhere in her soul she knew him. She'd never felt this kind of familiarity before, and she wasn't sure what to do about it.

"I'm sorry, there's no Julie Wheeler here," she began, ignoring Marge's now-you're-going-to-be-abducted look. "But—"

Marge nudged her again, harder, and she stopped.

The man's brow relaxed and the lost tourist look disappeared. "I thought this had to be wrong," he said with a chuckle, shaking his head and reaching for a small slip of paper from the back pocket of his jeans. "This is hardly ol' Carl's type of joint."

"Carl?" Joleen asked quickly. Her heartbeat accelerated. No way. There was no way this guy she'd practically had imaginary sex with was a friend of Carl's. Her luck wasn't that bad.

"Carl Landon," he said. An unspoken question lingered in the air.

The clock on the wall burned in the corner of Joleen's eye. It was three-thirty. Carl was supposed to have gotten there half an hour earlier and, now that she thought about it, it wasn't like him to be late. "Has something happened to Carl?" she asked, a little too loudly. *Did I jinx him by telling Marge I wasn't sure I wanted him? Did I foul up our relationship by being ridiculously attracted to a stranger when I'm supposed to be starting a future with Carl?*

The man's brow lifted again, and he shifted his weight, now regarding Joleen with some skepticism in his light green eyes. "Would it be fair to guess that now you *do* know Julie Wheeler?"

"I do if you mean *Joleen* Wheeler." She met his sardonic look with some heat, forgetting, for a moment, the draw she had just felt toward this man. "That would be me."

His eyes widened in what looked like genuine surprise for a moment before he quickly regained control and said, "I apologize for the mistake, Joleen. I can see how you might have been baffled as to who I meant when I asked for Julie."

The spark which only moments earlier had ignited between them fizzled like a match dunked in water. He was making fun of her.

She felt the heat rise in her face but ignored it. "What's this about Carl?" She swallowed hard. "He was supposed to meet me here half an hour ago—has there been an accident?"

"Nope. He had to take off for Monte Carlo this morning—business, of course." There was almost sarcasm behind that statement. "He asked me to come and take you back to the ranch, so..." He shrugged and splayed his arms. "That's what I'm doing. You ready?"

Joleen straightened, mentally digging her heels into the ground. "Who *are* you?"

"I'm Jake."

"Jake..?"

"His brother." He gave a brief smile, revealing the same impossibly straight white teeth as Carl's, but on Jake somehow they didn't quite seem so impossible. "Don't tell me he's never mentioned me," he said in a voice that said he wasn't the least bit surprised.

"He hasn't," Joleen said, frowning. Carl's *brother?* This was Carl's *brother?* The first stranger she ever feels instant lust for had to be Carl's brother? This was definitely a bad sign. "I don't think Carl's ever mentioned you," she said weakly.

"But the *National Intruder* sure has," Marge broke in, scratching her chin and nodding. She glanced at Joleen. "I *knew* I'd seen that face before." She turned back to Jake. "You're the black sheep Landon kid who joined up as a monk somewhere in Tibet."

Jake's smile returned, tinged with wry humor. "Rumors of my vows were greatly exaggerated. I just stayed for lunch, really."

Joleen noticed a subtle darkening in his eyes, then mentally chided herself for noticing. "I still don't get it, why did Carl send you instead of letting me know himself?"

He sucked air through his frozen smile and

shrugged again. "That's Carl." He looked behind her. "Are those your bags?" He started toward them.

"I can get them," Jo said, a little too quickly and a little too loudly.

He raised his hands as if in surrender. "Okay, okay. Didn't mean to insult you." He stopped. "I'll go pull the car up to the front door."

"But I have my own car." She wondered if her old clunker would make it all the way from Alvira to the western edge of Dallas. She'd been planning on riding out with Carl originally, because he'd insisted she use one of his cars when she got there. Something about not wanting to risk getting oil stains on the driveway. She could understand that. Well, she'd just take her car and park outside the driveway. That was better than sitting in a car with Jake Landon—or any stranger, she reasoned—all that time. "It's right there."

His gaze followed to where she pointed, then he looked back at her and cocked his head. "It's a long drive," he said doubtfully.

"I know that."

"It's going to be over a hundred degrees out today. That thing got air-conditioning?"

"Yes, of course." Immediately she could tell he knew better, so she added, as if it was what she'd meant all along, "When I roll all the windows down."

He looked at her for one charged instant, then nodded. "Okay, it's your choice. You can follow me."

She took a steadying breath after he turned to leave. "Perfect."

He regarded her in silence for a few more moments, perhaps waiting for her to give one last delicate protest so he could come to her rescue, then said, "I'll just go pull my car up out front then, so you can follow me out."

She nodded and took another breath after he turned to leave. "I'll be right out." She turned to Marge and said under her breath, "I don't like this one bit."

"Oh, go on," Marge hissed back. "And ride with him. You know you can't depend on your car."

"At the moment I have more confidence in my car than I do in—" she was going to say *myself* but she knew Marge would jump on that, so she said, "in some stranger I've never even heard of before."

"It's Carl's brother, what could happen to you?"

Joleen looked back at Jake leaving the diner. All she could see was the flattering fit of his jeans as he walked away and the way his shirt pulled at the shoulders and loosened at his trim waist. He couldn't have looked sexier if he'd tried.

"Nothing could happen," Joleen said, with less satisfaction than she would have liked. "Nothing."

Marge laid a gentle hand on Joleen's shoulder. "Listen, Jo, give this thing a chance. You're wound up as tight as a trussed turkey. Relax."

"It's difficult to relax knowing I could be making the biggest mistake of my life. Giving up my apartment was a big deal but giving up this..." She looked around and smiled. "I know it ain't much, but apart from night school these past few years, this place has pretty much been my whole world."

"And it'll always be here for you if you need it,"

Marge assured her. "You know you always have a job here and a home with me."

Joleen looked at her, but the tears burning in her eyes obscured her vision. "Thanks, Marge. That means a lot."

Marge sniffed loudly. "But you're not going to need to come back here, honey. You're gonna walk out that door and follow that man into your future."

"You mean—"

"I mean *now*. You never know what's going to happen until you try." She raised her eyebrow in a way that Joleen had long known meant there would be no arguments. "Now get on out there and send me a postcard from Dallas."

You never know what's going to happen until you try. It was true. It was a cliché, but it was true. Joleen squared her shoulders and looked out the door at Jake. "I'll go now," she said, turning back to Marge. "And I'll do my best to make it work."

Jake walked slowly to his Jeep and resisted the urge to look back at Joleen Wheeler and the greasy spoon she was about to emerge from. This was unbelievable. If this was a dream it was uncharacteristically surreal, even for him.

Something about her was so…what was the word? *Familiar.* For no good reason, he felt like he knew her, and he just *knew* Carl was underestimating her, that she had a lot more fire in her than Carl could see. But maybe Jake was completely wrong about her. It wouldn't be the first time he'd been wrong about people, and undoubtedly it wouldn't be the last.

He heaved a breath and allowed himself one glance back. The two women were hugging tightly by the door. He'd felt something the moment he'd laid eyes on Joleen—he could have sworn Carl had said *Julie*. It was the sort of attraction that happened across crowded rooms in old movies.

Her voice had the soothing timbre of a low-toned flute playing a lullaby. And her perfume had a light flower scent he recognized but couldn't identify. It had drawn him toward her, like a bee to the flower itself. But it wasn't just her voice, or her face, or the way she smelled. There was something else about her that made him want to be near her.

He forced the thought away. Why was he trying so hard to define it? It wasn't like it mattered; she was coming to the ranch for Carl. Hell, she was going to marry Carl, as impossible as that was to imagine.

The idea that Carl would go this far in his aspirations to become governor...Jake shook his head. What was it Carl had said? That he needed to find someone obscure, someone beautiful he could dress up and mold into whatever he wanted.

"Your typical small-town, all-American girl," he had said. "If I could 'rescue' a girl from poverty in a one-horse town, I'd be a hero to the working class."

It made sense in Carl's self-absorbed mind. The working class wasn't a constituency he would normally be popular with, to say the least. He was viewed as an oil magnate who was born into money and did little to earn it. That wasn't exactly true, but to many people using money to earn *more* money through interest and dividends—not to mention gambling—wasn't quite the same as *earning* it.

Jake stopped at his car door and turned back when he heard the tiny tinkle of the bells on the diner door. Joleen came out with one small tattered suitcase in her hand and a large leather purse over her shoulder. She didn't meet his eyes, so he was able to look at her more objectively than he had at first.

She was, he noticed now, built like the proverbial brick house. *Chunky,* his mother would have said in disparaging tones. Not what anyone would really call fat, but Joleen's figure was fuller than what was currently fashionable. It suited her. She would have looked odd if she were as rail thin as most of Carl's girlfriends. With hair so pale it was almost white, she looked exactly like a 1950s pinup girl. Yet she didn't play that up. Her simple skirt and modest short-sleeved shirt did nothing to emphasize her cleavage or shapely legs. Jake liked that. Better to leave some things to the imagination.

But now he didn't allow himself that moment of imagination he'd indulged in when he first saw her. Whatever Carl's reasons for getting involved with her, he *was* involved and Jake wasn't the kind of guy to look at another man's girl.

No matter how pretty she was. No matter how soft the expression in her eyes, or how full her lips were.

The pity of it was that she probably didn't know

what she was getting herself into. She probably had no idea what it was like to be Carl Landon's wife.

Jake could see what Carl had meant when he said Joleen had "potential." He hated that Svengali attitude, but he could see what Carl saw: Joleen had a beautiful face. No, it was more than just beautiful, it was *captivating*. She had that undefinable quality that makes movie stars legends; some inner glow that made it difficult to take your eyes off of her.

Her eyes were clear blue, and her brows arched over them in a way that made her look both open and intelligent. Her nose was straight and unremarkable, its most notable characteristic being that it lacked the artificial tilt and narrow tip that so many of the Dallas set had paid to have added. Her chin was strong in its set and slightly rounded. But Carl would probably starve that off her, Jake thought.

It was too bad, Jake thought again as he watched her turn and wave once more to the woman inside the door. This Joleen was probably a really nice girl. She had no idea her Cinderella dreams were leading her straight into the demolition of all the wishes she thought life with Carl would fulfill.

"I'm ready when you are," she said, pulling him out of his thoughts.

He looked at her old jalopy. The tire tread was nearly worn down on the rear tires, and the wind carried the faint scent of oil, as well as Joleen's sweet flowery perfume, from that direction. "You're sure you wouldn't rather just ride together?" he asked casually.

She obviously knew exactly what he was getting

at. She yanked open the rusty door of her car and tossed the suitcase and purse in, then turned to Jake with a slightly self-conscious shrug. "It gets me where I want to go." As if on cue, the side mirror slipped halfway off its mount.

Jake smiled. "Does it know you want to go a hundred and ten miles away?"

"It's a good old American-made car." She knocked the mirror back into place as she passed. "These things never die."

"There are plenty of lousy American cars."

She stopped at the driver's door and looked at him across the roof just long enough for him to notice her face had colored.

Immediately, he felt bad for having insulted her. "I've even had one or two troubles with old Bessie here." *Bessie?* Where the hell did that come from? Suddenly as nervous as a kid, he tapped his Jeep on the roof and the awkward silence extended.

"Well, I'll be behind you if you have any car trouble," Joleen said with a shadow of a smile. Jake couldn't tell if she was joking or reassuring him.

Whichever it was, he liked the way she said it.

He watched her climb into the car and, Jake could have sworn, tied her seat belt across her waist. She had to crank the engine three times before it finally turned over. When it did, Jake pulled out in front of her and started down the long highway toward Dallas.

Jake had the feeling that the asphalt line into Dallas was nothing compared to the other road ahead.

The one that might well define his future and his brotherly honor.

Because apart from his mother, who was nursing an ingrown toenail in her bedroom and probably would be for the next month, unless she decided to get off the eiderdown and go to Palm Beach, he and Joleen were going to be alone on the ranch together until Carl got back.

Chapter Two

"**S**tupid car," Jo muttered, grinding it into gear and pulling out onto the road. She rolled the window down and hot, damp air streamed in, lowering the saunalike heat only fractionally. The heat was a great metaphor for the emotional quandary she found herself in now. Sweat beaded immediately on her forehead.

She glanced in the rearview mirror and rolled her eyes at the overweight, overheated woman she saw. "Well, I've made a great impression on Carl's family so far." She noticed, thanks to weeks of Carl's hounding, the long *I* sound of her Texas drawl when she said *great*.

"It's not grite," Carl had insisted, "it's great. Repeat after me: great, late, date, fate."

"Great," she said to herself out loud, and smiled. "It's *great* that my *fate* was to date—" she hesitated "—Carl." It seemed like it should have rhymed and for one insane moment she thought maybe the fact that it didn't was an omen.

Casting that idea away, she read the license plate on the car in front of her. "Jake." She sighed. "Okay, Jake, so I didn't make the best impression on you so far. Nothing's lost, there's still time." She repositioned her hands on the steering wheel and tightened her grip. "I can do this, I can do it. I can make Carl happy. I can learn to be as classy and poised as anyone."

As she drove along behind Jake, she recalled that several times Carl had mentioned his brother, but never by name. She wondered why. There had been no bitterness in his voice, or any indication that there had been a falling out. It was almost as if he didn't think Jake was important enough to warrant the time it took to say his name.

That gave her pause. So how much had Carl talked about her, if Jake thought her name was Julie? She pushed the thought from her mind. It may have reflected on Carl's relationship with Jake, but it certainly didn't reflect on his relationship with Joleen or his feelings for her. Why would he be pushing to marry her if he didn't completely adore her?

Why are you considering marrying him when you don't completely adore him? a small voice nagged at her.

"I've been very frank with him about my feelings," she answered the voice. "Or the fact that I'm unsure of my feelings. He's the one who insisted I move out here for the summer and integrate into the family."

But you're doing it because everyone else wants you to.

"I'm also doing it because *I* want to. I'm doing it because if I keep going at the rate I'm going it's going to take me another twelve years to finish school and make something of my life. I'm doing it because Carl's a really nice guy and I like him a lot, and there might be a future there for us."

What, you, as a political wife? You'd be miserable!

"That's not necessarily true." She'd given this considerable thought already. "In that position, I could do a lot to help people. I could do a lot of good. And I could have children, raise a family and know I'd be able to feed and clothe them."

It occurred to her that if Jake looked at her in his rearview mirror, this talking to herself wasn't going to do much to enhance his impression of her. But the voice persisted.

What about being in love?

This one always stumped her. "Love...there are lots of different kinds of love. Love is respect and camaraderie." She didn't quite buy that but sometimes when she said it firmly enough she *almost* believed it. "Anyway, being in love is overrated. Everyone says it wears off, anyway." But her conscience railed at this one, as always. It was one thing for her to choose to live in a marriage like that, but it was quite another to let Carl in for that.

She turned on the radio to stop the conversation in her head. There was a weather report predicting thunderstorms and a tornado watch. She changed the channel and Stephen Stills advised, "Love the one you're with." She pushed another button and settled for an old song about a train.

That she could live with.

Jake signaled a turn onto the highway, and Joleen held her breath for a moment. This was the test for this old car. The outside temperature was nearly one hundred degrees and it was going to get hotter before it got cooler. She glanced at the heat gauge; it was in the normal range. She let out her breath. It would be okay.

Jake drew smoothly into traffic, immediately accelerating to the speed limit. Joleen crushed the pedal to the floor and prayed for enough speed to get her out of the way of the oncoming traffic. The car rattled and bucked in response.

It had to make it all the way to Dallas, it just had to. Suddenly it felt like her independence depended on it.

There are plenty of lousy American cars, Jake had said. She had to grant him that. You didn't see many of these old things on the road these days. But that didn't give him the right to make fun of her car. She wished she'd had the nerve to point that out instead of standing there stupidly, letting him insult her.

Unfortunately, standing by politely while people were rude was a hard habit to break, and her mother had worked hard to teach her that lesson in civility. It had been so hard sometimes to see how customers treated her mom—harder than it had ever been to take the same treatment when she started waiting tables. She felt a pang and realized how sad her mother would have been if she'd thought Joleen would live the same life. Helen Wheeler had worked hard all those years to give Joleen what she believed would be a better life.

It would have broken her heart to know that the $8,000 she'd scrimped and saved barely covered her own burial costs.

"I know that wasn't quite what you had in mind for that money, Mama." Joleen heard her voice break, and swallowed the lump that had formed in her throat. "It was a beautiful funeral, though." She left it at that.

Yes, her mother would be proud of her now. That a Landon had not only taken an interest in her but actually wanted her to marry him!

So who did she think she was, telling him to wait while she considered it? The rest of the world would probably think she was nuts.

At least she had the integrity to make sure marriage was the best thing for both of them. No matter what Marge said, love was a necessary ingredient to marriage.

Jake signaled and Joleen followed him into the center lane, and she thought again of her instant and intense attraction to him. Surely that had only been a trick of the mind. Or maybe it was proof that she'd fit in with the Landons because she felt so immediately familiar around them.

That was good.

She sighed. Even this back view of Jake's silhouette drew her attention. He was so different from Carl. She thought about her first impression of Jake when he'd walked into the Hometown Diner. He didn't have the straight, wholly symmetrical good looks of Carl, but there was something even more charming about the small bump on his nose and his slightly crooked smile. And his eyes—the color wasn't that different but the expression was almost enough to distinguish them as different species. Where Carl radiated confidence and an outgoing personality, Jake's eyes were full of thought. He reminded Joleen of a poet. There was trouble in his soul and you could see it right in his eyes.

Unfortunately she'd always found that irresistible.

Until now, that was. She could resist it because this was a momentary lapse, due to the enormity of the idea of marriage. She would keep reminding herself of that, and soon she would believe it.

Wait a minute. She thumped her hands against the steering wheel. This attraction to Jake wasn't because of him, it was because he reminded her of Carl. Of course that was it! It had been a couple of weeks since she'd seen Carl, and she missed him. Sometimes people missed other people without really realizing it. Then, when they saw someone who resembled them, it all came flooding back, sometimes transferring under the guise of physical attraction.

That could happen.

Breathing easier now, Joleen assured herself that was all she was feeling. It boded *well* for her relationship with Carl, actually.

But just to be on the safe side she was going to avoid Jake as much as possible when they got to the ranch. Carl would probably be in tomorrow, and they would be spending most of their time together or with his parents and whoever else lived at the ranch. If television soap operas were any indication, there were always tons of people living on these big estates.

Except, of course, Carl at the moment. When had he left the country? Why hadn't he told her? Jake had said it was a last-minute thing, so if he'd gone today, *would* he be back tomorrow?

Of course he will, don't be silly, she told herself. The notion that he would have her come out and then leave and not spend any time with her was preposterous. He wasn't the sort of guy to leave her stranded in a strange place with people she'd never met before.

No, he wasn't that sort of guy, she thought, and felt herself relax somewhat against her seat.

Maybe she could marry Carl Landon. She would give it her best shot. The dream was still alive and it was going to come true for Joleen and for her late mother. Heck, maybe she could even have Marge come out for long stays on the ranch. Or—she was getting excited now—Marge could move in and help with the children when they had them eventually.

Comforted, Joleen increased her pressure on the accelerator. The sooner they got there the better. The car engine whined in protest.

"Please," she prayed, "please, please, please keep going." She glanced heavenward. "Really, Mama, I'm going to give this my best shot, don't you worry. I'll give it every chance—"

Before she could finish her sentence, a small explosion jerked the car to the side.

Without thinking, Joleen tried to downshift and found the clutch had locked. She pressed her foot against the brake and the car shuddered hard. With a pounding heart she coasted the car onto the shoulder. The engine wound down to a halt almost as soon as she was clear of traffic.

She sat for a moment, stunned, still clutching the wheel. Then she heard a small hiss and noticed a stream of smoke trailing up from under the hood. She shouted a word her mother wouldn't have been proud to hear her say and pulled the hood release lever. Within seconds she had grabbed the fire extinguisher from the back seat, and jumped from the car.

Holding the fire extinguisher in front of her with one hand like a shield, Joleen ran to the front of the car and nudged the hood up with her other hand. Nothing was on fire. She looked more closely.

It was worse than she'd feared.

The fan had broken loose and cut through the transmission and the radiator. The tear was huge and jagged. The parts would have to be replaced, not repaired. And that would take not only time, but money.

She looked at the road ahead and practically saw Jake's dust. He was long gone. She was going to have to get a bus or, worse, a cab for the rest of the way. All her money was in her bank account, and even that only amounted to a couple hundred dollars.

The radiator was sputtering drops of green liquid,

and hissing in what sounded to Joleen like a self-satisfied way.

The timing could not have been worse.

"I gotta tell you, car, this really seems deliberate." She shook her head and turned to look at the traffic rushing by. Of course there was still no sign of Jake ahead. It would probably be thirty miles before he realized she wasn't behind him anymore. That is, if he realized it at all.

"Couldn't you have gone just a little further?" she said to the car. "Half an hour more. Forty-five minutes at the most." The engine smelled of burning oil. The way today was going it was probably a matter of minutes before the entire car blew up, sending her flying right into Oklahoma.

Imagine the cab fare *then*, she thought and had to laugh.

Far in the distance she could see an overpass. With any luck at all there would be a phone there and she could call a tow truck. That way at least the car would get a ride. She wasn't sure how she was going to get out to Carl's ranch now, but she was more determined than ever to do it.

This was a sign.

She couldn't live this way anymore. Everything was a struggle. She tossed the fire extinguisher onto the back seat of the car and grabbed her purse from the front seat. This was an omen of some sort. What had she been thinking about right before the engine blew? Well, it didn't matter. This was proof positive that she couldn't keep moving through life at this pace. For every step she took forward, it felt like she took ten steps back.

"Stop thinking that way," she told herself, as she started walking toward the overpass. "Don't be so negative. There have been a lot of good days, too. There's a positive side to everything." She thought, hard, then shook her head. "But sometimes you really have to search for it."

She wiped an arm across her damp brow and wondered how long she would have to search for the positive side of this before finally admitting that it was absolutely horrible and totally unfair.

A passing trucker blasted his horn and gave her the thumbs-up sign.

Not much longer.

A car whooshed up behind her and she heard the emergency brake crank on. A door opened and shut and a man called, "Come on, let me give you a ride."

Joleen picked up her pace. Fear coursed through her. She'd seen news stories about what happened to women alone on highways when their cars broke down. She didn't turn around, didn't want to make eye contact with whoever it was.

Running steps clopped up behind her and she felt adrenaline surge through her body.

A hand clamped down on her shoulder. "Joleen!"

She whirled around to find Jake standing there. "Where did you come from?"

"Originally? Lubbock." He put his hands up. "I know what you're thinking, but Buddy Holly wasn't the only guy born there."

She would have laughed but something about Jake made her a nervous wreck. "I mean, how did you get behind me?" she asked, thinking she should respond to the Buddy Holly thing but coming up short. "I thought you'd be miles away by now."

"You almost sound like you wish I was."

"No, I didn't mean—"

"It's a hell of a walk from here," he said, a little shortly. Then he smiled, but stopped just shy of actually looking happy. "And, no offense, but you're already sort of wilting. Come on and get in."

Her face grew warm and she realized that now she was flushed red on top of being sweaty and "wilted." "I have to call a tow truck," she said, as if she'd been in such a hurry to do it that she hadn't the time to stop and get into his car.

"I already called one."

Joleen hesitated, wondering at her impulse to refuse Jake's help, when it was so obviously the only answer. It wasn't like she could tell him she preferred to walk and she'd meet him at the gas station five miles ahead. "Thanks," she said, annoyed with herself for not sounding like she meant it. She tried again. "I really appreciate it."

They started walking back toward his car.

"Anytime." They got to the Jeep and Jake met her eyes.

For one long moment neither of them spoke and Joleen felt her heart beating so that she thought it might burst. *Stop it!* she told herself. *Calm down, this is ridiculous!*

"I really hate to trouble you like this," she said.

He cocked his head and gave a slight smile. "It's no trouble at all, Joleen."

She liked the way he said her name, with the emphasis on the "leen" part, instead of the country thick *Jo*leen. He was a class act. Just like his brother.

He opened the car door. "Hop in."

She paused, avoiding his eyes which she knew were trained on her, then climbed into the Jeep with a silent prayer that she would live through the next hour without making a complete fool of herself.

Chapter Three

Joleen leaned back on the cool leather seat. Jake got in and turned the engine on. The air-conditioning blasted deliciously against her face. "I didn't mean to sound ungrateful before, but how *did* you get here so fast?" she asked. "I thought you'd be in Dallas before you realized I wasn't behind you anymore."

"I was keeping an eye on you," he answered. "When I saw you pull over, I took the next exit and came back around." He paused. "And darlin'," he glanced into her eyes, "you sure as hell don't have to be *grateful* to me for coming back for you."

Embarrassment flooded her again and she didn't know what to say. *Thank you* sprang to her lips but she pressed them shut. Then she remembered she'd only taken her purse from the car. "My suitcase—"

"I grabbed it before we left, it's in the back." He jerked his head toward the back seat and she looked. The ratty old thing looked like an insult against the glove leather seat. "You sure that's all you want to take with you? It can't be much, that bag doesn't weigh more than a few pounds."

That's all I have. "I try to travel light."

He must have read her mind because he looked a little embarrassed and said, "Good policy." He nodded and looked back at the road, tapping his fingers against the steering wheel.

Joleen looked at his hands. They were worker's hands, with calluses and cracks. His fingers were long and tapered, his nails short. Those calluses would feel rough against smooth skin, Joleen mused. It probably added a whole new dimension to sex. Who knew what magic he worked with those hands? They looked strong, capable of just about anything. Not at all like Carl's soft skin and manicured nails.

Of course, it was important to Carl's job for him to look neat and professional at all times. Dirt under his fingernails maybe detracted from that image. She wondered if Jake had to worry about his image, too.

"What do you do?" Joleen asked him. "For a living, I mean."

"You serious?"

"Of course." She frowned. "Why, is there some joke here that I don't know about?"

"No, it's just funny you should ask me that." He shook his head. "You know, no one ever asks me that question."

"No? Why not?"

He shrugged. "I guess they think I live off family money, sitting around all day playing, I don't know, backgammon.'' He laughed. ''Or shuttlecock.'' He glanced at her and added, ''I don't.''

She smiled. ''Well, your family wealth isn't exactly a secret.'' She regretted her candor the minute the words were out of her mouth. ''I guess people assume you're in the oil business.'' *Which you probably are, God, I'm such an idiot.*

He glanced at her with surprise in his expression. ''The family wealth has nothing to do with me.'' His tone was strange, as though there was something more to this, perhaps something that she should already know.

''What do you mean?''

''You don't know?'' He studied her eyes for a moment, glanced back at the road, then back at Joleen. ''I was disinherited years ago. Before my father died.''

Her shock must have shown in her face because he laughed and added, ''It's okay with me, believe me.''

Joleen was nearly speechless. ''I'm sorry,'' she mustered. ''I didn't know. I certainly didn't mean to bring up bad memories.''

He guided the car smoothly onto an exit ramp and said, ''You didn't. I'm proud of the fact that I make my own way in life. I don't think the old man knew it but he did me a favor.''

''Do you mean that?'' Could he possibly mean it? Who would be glad to lose millions of dollars and have to struggle for a living? Good Lord, Joleen would do almost anything to alleviate even *part* of the struggle.

"I mean it," Jake said, with a smile in his voice. "But everyone finds it hard to believe."

Joleen did, too, but he sounded earnest. "But you do still live at the house?" she asked. Surely that was a given.

"Only for the moment." A heavy silence dropped between them. "I just sold my place in Fort Worth. When I'm through here I'm going to head north, find myself a piece of land, maybe in Wyoming or Montana."

Joleen nodded, but inside she felt a burning curiosity about the circumstances surrounding his family quarrel. The idea of an heir being disinherited and stuck with that lot because the disinheritor had died was bad enough, but the fact that he'd become a drifter, with no real home and only the vaguest of plans, seemed…the first word she thought of was *tragic*, but that was wrong. Clearly there was nothing tragic about Jake Landon.

He cleared his throat and fidgeted his hands on the steering wheel. "I hope I haven't disillusioned you, or shattered some idyllic picture of the Landon family sipping tea at poolside."

She shrugged. "I couldn't quite picture it, anyway. Not you, that is. You don't seem the type."

He raised an eyebrow. "Are you good at that? Figuring people out, I mean."

Did he sense she'd been doing that with him since the minute she'd seen him? "Sometimes. I mean, there are certain things that just make sense when you look at a person. For instance, I'd guess you do a lot of work outdoors, which is why I asked."

He looked interested. "How can you tell I work outdoors?"

"Your hands, for one thing. You've got calluses on calluses." She glanced self-consciously at her own hands and slipped them to her sides.

He looked at his hands for a moment, then back at the road. "How did you know I got these from working and not from a rough day sailing on the Caribbean?"

She considered. "In that case they would be blisters and would probably hurt like the devil."

"How do you know they don't?"

"You don't move gingerly, like every touch hurts."

"Some do," he said, without taking his eyes from the road.

It was obviously a loaded statement but Joleen didn't dare ask him to elaborate, particularly after inadvertently dragging his family problems out of him.

After a quiet moment he said, "So you've done pretty well so far. What do you think I do for a living?"

Joleen smiled, trying to lighten the mood. "I think you play backgammon and shuttlecock outside all day on some Caribbean beach."

He laughed and the sound was so unexpected that she started. It was such a nice laugh—sincere in a way Carl's seldom was. She wished she could make Carl laugh that way. She was going to try harder from now on.

"What about you, have you worked in that restaurant for long?"

"Technically I've worked there four years," she said. "But I pretty much grew up there. My mom worked there until she died."

"I'm sorry," Jake said. "That must be hard."

"It is." Her voice was quiet. She cleared her throat and went on. "Anyway, I took over her job when she passed away."

"What did you do until then?"

She sighed and looked out at the traffic whizzing by. "Oh, this and that. I'd had two years of college at the time she died but two years of studying architecture doesn't get you very far. I've finished another semester's worth of courses since then but I started late—twenty-four—so it's real slow going now."

He smiled and she felt encouraged. "Slow and steady, they say…"

"Well, it's slow but it hasn't been steady."

"What'd you do before college?"

She stretched her legs out as much as she could in the little cab. "Before that I worked to earn enough money to start college. First I worked at the Giddyup Grocery Store, and then at a child care center in town. That was the best."

For some reason he suddenly looked puzzled. "You like kids?"

"Oh, I love them," she said enthusiastically. "I can't wait to have my own someday."

"Huh." He kept his eyes straight ahead, but Joleen could tell he was musing over that fact as if it had some unexpected significance.

"Don't you like kids?" she asked, at a loss.

"Me?" He looked surprised. "Sure, I like kids a lot. But I was thinking of Carl."

"What about Carl?"

He shrugged vaguely. "You know, Carl and kids..."

Carl and kids? What, was he allergic to children? The father of six already? "I don't know what you're talking about, what about Carl and kids?"

He hesitated. "Nothing. I'm sure you all have talked about it. It's none of *my* business— Well, look at that!" He pointed out the window.

Joleen looked. The landscape hadn't changed a bit, it was all cars, guardrail and fields. "What?" she asked. "I don't see anything."

"Thought I saw a...bald eagle," he fumbled. "Never mind."

She looked again. There was nothing in the sky above, not even a cloud. She squinted and looked harder. An *eagle?* Was this guy okay to drive? "I don't see anything."

"Must have been a mistake," he said dismissively. Clearly he didn't want to talk about the child thing, but Joleen made a mental note to ask Carl himself.

Neither one spoke for a few minutes.

"You never answered my question," Joleen said, after a bit.

"What question was that?"

"About what you do, if you're not with Landon Industries."

He slapped the blinker down and guided the Jeep

smoothly into the left lane. "At the moment I am with Landon Industries. I'm on the board and there's a meeting coming up. A vote."

"I see."

"But I also breed horses for a living. I've got twenty or thirty Thoroughbreds at the ranch right now."

"Oh." She nodded but it hadn't occurred to her that there might be horses to ride on the ranch. She thought "ranch" was just a label to some people, like "homestead." "So there are horses there?"

"About a hundred and ten of them all together." He looked at her. "You ride?"

"I haven't since I was about ten and my uncle had an old mare he let me ride on weekends." She hadn't thought about that in years. "I loved it. But it's been ages."

"Well, now's your chance to ride again if you want to." Jake looked at Joleen, and she thought she saw in his eyes that he couldn't believe the conversation had grown so lame.

She looked out the window again. Skyscrapers loomed in the distance. They must be getting close now. She wasn't sure whether she was eager to have the ride over with, because she wouldn't be having this forced conversation with Jake anymore, or whether she was dreading the end of the ride, because that meant the intimidating task of meeting the rest of the family, staff and whoever else lived on the ranch. All without Carl there to guide her through it.

She took a deep breath, inhaling the yummy bay

rum scent of Jake's aftershave and was grateful for that small comfort at least.

Suddenly a loud ringing reverberated through the small car. Joleen gasped.

"Phone," Jake said. "It's probably the garage calling with news about your car." He flipped a switch on the dashboard. "Yep?"

"Jake?"

It was Carl's voice coming out of the speaker! Joleen decided the surge of adrenaline she felt was a positive thing. Excitement.

"It's me," Jake said. "Where are you?"

"Where do you think I am, I'm at the Casino d'Azure with Sabri—"

"Joleen's with me," Jake interrupted, inordinately loud.

"I know that," Carl snapped. "That's why I'm calling."

"I mean she's here. Right next to me." Jake was enunciating carefully. "Her car broke down so she's riding with me."

"Her *car* broke down?" Carl asked. His concern should have been touching but it just missed. "Damn it, I *knew* something like this would happen if I wasn't there to take care of things myself." He sighed heavily. "Put her on."

"She's on, bro. You're on the speaker, the handset broke again."

There was a moment of silence, then Carl said jovially, "Joleen! Sweetheart, baby, how are you?"

Sweetheart, baby? What was going on? Carl didn't normally talk to her that way. For the hundredth time that day, Joleen felt the heat rise in her cheeks. She looked at Jake, then down at the dash for whatever microphone it was that would pick up her voice.

Jake pointed to what looked like a small speaker and Joleen leaned awkwardly toward it.

"F-fine, Carl. I'm fine. How are you? How's France?"

"Monaco," Carl corrected, "is beautiful. I wish you could have come with me, but..." He let the sentence dangle and so did she.

She leaned toward the speaker again. The seat belt cut uncomfortably into her waist. "When are you comin' back?"

"Soon. I'm com*ing* soon." The subtle correction irked her. "Don't you worry. You just enjoy yourself in Dallas. Get to know people. Mother should be able to put you in contact with all the people who matter. I was thinking you could work on the charity ball committee."

"Great," Joleen said, without much enthusiasm.

"Ay-ay-ay," Carl's voice piped through the tiny speaker. "Pronounce that ay, *great*."

Face burning, she looked at Jake's profile and thought he was all but rolling his eyes.

"Sweetheart?" Carl's voice called out, small and cartoonish from the speaker. "Are you there?"

"I'm here," Joleen said.

"I miss you."

She wasn't used to making personal declarations in front of other people. "Well...you'll be back soon."

"Yes, I will. You just hold on to that thought. How's the ring, still sparkling?"

Her hand automatically flew to her pocket. The ring was still there. "It's like new," she told him honestly.

"Good. I'm glad to hear you're enjoying it."

He was easily satisfied, that Carl. He heard what he wanted to hear. "Yes, well—"

Carl interrupted again, "All right, I'd better go now. Some of the gentlemen I've come to see are coming to the table. I'll call you later, okay? 'Bye."

There was a click and a buzz before she had a chance to say a word. Jake reached down and flipped the switch off, heaving a breath as he did so.

"Sounds like he's having a good time," Joleen commented carefully.

"Yes," Jake said, without inflection. "He did."

An awkward moment passed.

Yup, that's about all there is to say about that. Joleen sighed and concentrated on smoothing imaginary wrinkles out of her skirt.

Several miles passed in silence with only the periodic clicking of the tires over the joints in the road. Joleen was more acutely aware of Jake's presence than she had ever been of anyone else's. She'd never been great at maintaining conversation with strangers. Taking a lunch order, giving the time, gabbing about the weather, all of that she could do. But this...she sighed and looked at Jake: his legs, his waist, his broad chest, his arms, his strong but sensitive hands, his uneven—but somehow very nice—profile. She sighed again.

The silence continued, and Joleen took out her purse and pretended to search for something. Anything to keep her busy. Her hand brushed across a chocolate candy bar and she stopped. Nothing would taste better right now, but she had to lose weight. After all, as Carl kept telling her, she would be in the public eye, under scrutiny at times.

She withdrew her hand and set the purse down, trying to push away the craving she was now feeling.

It takes twenty minutes for a food craving to pass, she told herself. Where had she read that? Oh well, she hoped it was true.

After several minutes, the phone rang again.

Jake reached down and flipped the switch. "Yeah, Jake Landon here."

"Jake, it's Carl again. Let me talk to Joleen."

A muscle ticked in Jake's jaw. "You *are.*"

"Oh, that's right, you broke the handset. How'd you do that, anyway?"

Jake looked decidedly aggravated. "Look, Carl, it's your dime, didn't you call across the ocean to talk to Joleen?"

"Yes, I did. Joleen, you there?"

"Yes?"

"I need you to do me a favor, do you mind?"

Something about the way he asked made her uncomfortable. She shifted in her seat. "N-no. Of course not, what is it?"

"I forgot about a park opening on a piece of land in the city. It's for underprivileged kids, I think." He paused. "Maybe it's Greenpeace. You can ask my secretary. Anyway, I was supposed to make an appearance there tomorrow but I can't. Would you, as my fiancée, go in my place?''

"Oh, I don't know." That would be dishonest. She wasn't at all sure she was going to marry him, and going as his fiancée when she knew she wasn't would be a lie. "It really doesn't feel like it's my place to do that. I mean, who am I? I'm just ordinary. I'm one of them, I'm not a celebrity like you."

"Darling, you're my fiancée—"

They had to stay clear on this one point or she would suffocate. "No, Carl, I'm not—"

"Don't be modest." He clipped her off neatly. "I really need you to do this for me." He didn't seem the least bit self-conscious that Jake could hear every word they were saying to each other. "You know I wouldn't ask if it wasn't important."

Guilt flushed over her. "Of course, it's just that—"

"Have I ever asked you for anything before?"

"Well, no, but that's not what I was trying to say." Conversations like this were difficult enough over the phone without the added distraction of having to yell into a dashboard, with someone sitting not two feet away. "I'd just feel like a fake going there in your place like that."

"Sweetheart." Carl let the word drift in the air for a moment, and it mingled with Jake's bay rum aftershave. "Come on." Now Carl's voice had a firmer edge to it. He was coming in for the kill and she knew it. "It's not like you have to talk or anything. In fact, I don't want you to say anything. You just need to smile and look pretty.'' He hesitated. ''This is *important*.''

''Okay then,'' Joleen agreed, against her better judgment. She was starting to feel a little panicky. She thought again about the candy bar in her purse. ''If you think I can do any good.''

''Terrific! I knew I could count on you. I've already talked to Mother about teaching you the ropes. She'll tell you everything you need to know, so it's important that you listen to her advice. Now, go into Neiman-Marcus this afternoon and get something to wear—put it on my account. I'll call now and tell them you're going to be in.''

''But I brought clothes,'' Joleen protested. Her breathing felt tight.

He laughed. ''Throw them out. Get all new clothes, anything you want. Think Cinderella.''

She knew he meant it in a kind way, but still she felt flattened, like she'd been run over by a bulldozer. ''I think Cinderella was better off before she pretended to be someone she wasn't.'' The words were out before she could stop them, but once said, she felt a little better.

Carl evidently didn't hear her. ''Oops, gotta run now, babe. Have a good time at Neiman's.'' He chuckled. ''Like it or not you're going to have to get used to having the finer things in life.'' The now-familiar click and buzz sounded.

''I'm not sure I like it,'' Joleen said under her breath, then quickly looked up.

Jake didn't say anything, but she was certain he'd heard her.

He turned onto an off ramp and stopped at the stoplight at the end.

A few minutes passed in charged silence before Jake finally spoke.

"So," he said, looking directly into her eyes. He gestured at the phone speaker. "What's a girl like you doing with a guy like that?"

Chapter Four

Joleen stiffened, and Jake immediately wished he hadn't said anything.

"What did you say?" she asked sharply.

Jake shook his head. "Sorry." He knew it didn't sound sincere, but it was the best he could do. Part of him wanted to warn her off Carl right now, but another part didn't want to get involved. He'd learned long ago that the further he stayed away from Carl and his affairs, the happier he was.

Besides, if he tried to dissuade every bimbo and gold digger from getting involved with Carl, he'd never have time to do anything else. And it was unlikely that he could change any of their minds anyway—they knew what they were getting into. It was a calculated risk. Who was to say Joleen was any different from the rest of them?

His gut instinct, that's who.

"I shouldn't have said anything," he said lamely,

wishing she'd let it drop, but at the same time knowing for sure that she wouldn't.

"But you did," she persisted. "You asked what I was doing with 'a guy like that.' What did you mean?"

The war between honesty and discretion, involvement and detachment, raged in Jake. "I meant that you can do what you want," he evaded. "You don't have to do everything Carl instructs."

"I don't think he was *instructing*..."

"You don't?"

"No, I don't." Her voice rose slightly. "He only asked me to do him a favor."

Honesty and discretion called a truce. This was Carl's fiancée, and she was Carl's problem, not Jake's. If Joleen wanted to run headlong into a life sentence with his brother, that was her business. Jake wouldn't lie, but he wouldn't go far out of his way to protect Carl, either. He'd just try to mind his own business. "Okay, okay, I'm sorry. I shouldn't have said anything," he said, hoping she'd let it go.

Her gaze burned a hole in his cheek. "But...?"

"But what?"

"That's what *I* want to know." Her charming Texas twang increased with her ire. "I can tell you haven't said your piece, so why don't you go on and have done with it!"

Jake tried to contain his smile. Not only did her accent thicken when she was hot, but so did the down-home expressions.

"Are you laughing at me?" she asked.

"No." He looked at her and felt his heart warm

at her plaintive gaze. "Look, all I'm saying is it didn't sound like Carl *asking* for a favor to me, it sounded like a command." He shrugged. "What you do with it is your business."

"Oh." She sat back in her seat. "Well, you're mistaken. It's that simple."

"Hmm. I don't think it sounded like asking to you, either." Now why did he say that? Here he was, striving for detachment, and instead he dove head-long into involvement with a loaded statement like that.

"You don't know what I think," Joleen retorted.

He looked at her. Her blue eyes were sharp, and pink had risen in her pale cheeks. "No, you're right. I have no idea what you think." *Damned if I know why I care.* He looked back at the road, and turned the car onto the long, narrow road that led to the ranch.

Silence hovered between them like a fog. Several miles passed without a word between them. By the time he pulled into the driveway, Jake thought he'd never been so glad to face the old homestead.

Joleen opened her door the minute the car stopped and climbed out. "Thanks for the ride," she said, a little stiffly. "I do appreciate it."

"No problem." He looked at her across the top of the car. She was attractive when she was mad. Anger sharpened the intelligence in her eyes, replacing the lost puppy look she'd had for most of the trip. Not that he gave a damn, one way or the other.

"I apologize for losing my temper earlier," Joleen

said, with all the sincerity in the world. "I don't know what got into me."

His chest constricted. He couldn't care for this girl, he absolutely *could not* do it. "Joleen," he liked the way her name rolled off his tongue, "if that's losing your temper you're going to be—" he was going to say *eaten alive* but he thought better of it "—surprised by life in the city."

She met and held his eyes for a few seconds, then bent down and tried to wrestle the seat forward so she could get her suitcase from the back.

"Let me help you with that," he said, walking around the car to her side. "It's a little tricky." He reached around her, and she stepped back into him accidentally. Automatically his hand caught her at her waist to keep them both from stumbling. He groaned inwardly. The warmth of her body against the length of his sent a tremor across his chest. Her clothes smelled of crisp-scented laundry detergent. It was familiar, like her perfume, but he couldn't recall why. It didn't matter; what mattered was that he was thinking about it at all.

He had to get away from her.

But it was she who moved, side-stepping awkwardly. "Sorry," she said, without making eye contact.

"It's all right." Jake tightened his jaw and gave the seat release a rough jerk. The seat sprang forward. He grabbed her suitcase and pulled it out in one fluid motion, kicking the door shut with his knee. "This way," he tossed over his shoulder. He didn't mean for his voice to sound so cold but he wouldn't want to give anyone the idea that he was soft on Joleen.

She followed, her expression bemused. "Where is everyone?"

"Everyone?" He stopped. "What do you mean?"

"The people who live here, the staff..."

So Carl hadn't really prepared her for this at all. That figured. Jake went to the front door, trying not to feel sorry for Joleen. "The staff is off until next week," he opened the door, "and as for the people who live here, until Carl gets back, that's just you and me. And—"

"Jake?" The shrill cry of Virginia Landon echoed through the hall, as it seemed to every time he set foot in the door. One of these days he was going to look for the hidden sensor that always told her it was him. "Is that you, darling?"

Jake looked into Joleen's alarmed eyes. "And Mother," he finished, thinking the coolness of his tone made him sound a little too much like Norman Bates. "It's me," he called back, then to Joleen, added, "She's been laid up for the past couple of days with some sort of...toe...thing."

"Do you have Carl's young lady with you?" Virginia called again. Whatever else might ail her, he thought cynically, there was nothing wrong with those lungs.

He was glad to see the objection spring to Joleen's lips, but disappointed when she pressed them together instead of voicing it. She looked at him and he raised his eyebrows. "You ready to meet her?"

Joleen's face went white. "Oh, I don't want to…that is, if she's ill…"

He shook his head with a laugh. "You can't get out of it that easily." He shifted the weight of Joleen's suitcase and walked down the hall. "But I'll take you to your suite first and you can meet her when you're ready."

"Jake?" Virginia called again.

"She's here. I'm going to show her around first. You can meet her after a while." Without waiting for the argument that was sure to come, he took Joleen through the maze of hallways that led to what the family had always called "the little suite."

Carl had originally intended for her to take one of the more lavish suites in the east wing, but as soon as he'd gone, Virginia had changed things around. It was the beginning of much antagonism, Jake was sure. Poor Joleen had no idea that she already had the great matriarch's animosity. No one was good enough for Carl, in his mother's eyes, especially not someone who had come from the "wrong side of the tracks."

Like the Landons had. Jake and Carl's father had been a Lithuanian immigrant who'd made good after the stock market crash of '29. John Landowskas had been a kind man, and proud of his heritage. Virginia and Carl, on the other hand, had spent the last several decades trying to hide it.

Ironic, Jake thought, since Carl's own heritage would probably be as endearing to the voting public as his marriage to a poor girl from a tiny town. Probably. Then again, maybe he was wrong. After all,

Jake had a much better sense of people than he did of politics.

Politics were Carl's problem. So was his politically correct marriage to Joleen. Jake was staying out of it. He'd have to remember that.

"Where do you stay?" Joleen asked behind him, startling him out of his thoughts. "Is your room upstairs?"

"I stay out in the guest house."

They walked into her room and he noticed, now, that the guest house was clearly visible from the picture window by her bed. "There." He pointed vaguely, subconsciously measuring the distance between her bed and his to be about a hundred yards. For some reason this made his heart thud stupidly.

"Right there?"

"Right there." He set the suitcase down and waved an arm about the room. "Here's your foyer, bathroom, den, and there's a small kitchenette down the hall." He gestured vaguely and added, "Bedroom."

"Great." Joleen shifted her weight and looked out the window.

Jake searched for something else to say. "Feel free to use the phone for whatever."

She turned to him. "How do I get you?"

"What?" He glanced at her quickly.

She colored immediately. "I mean, how do I find you if—if Carl wants you...for some reason."

"Carl knows how to get ahold of me as long as I'm here. Oh, and there is a housekeeper. You can get her by dialling 01. Or is it 02?'' He considered. "I think it's 01. And the guest house is 04.''

"Thanks,'' Joleen said, a little breathlessly. She looked around, then said, "You said 'as long as I'm here.' Are you leaving? I mean, are you leaving the ranch?''

"Yes, I'm leaving.'' Was that hope in her voice? No, of course not. She didn't have any reason to feel one way or the other about his being there. It was probably just idle curiosity. Maybe even a matter of just being polite. "In just about two weeks and two days.''

"Just about?''

He sighed and leaned against the door frame. "I keep thinking Carl would have warned you, or given you some idea of what's going on here, but he didn't.''

She took a step backward. "*Warned* me? Are you dangerous?'' She tried to laugh, but it was a small attempt, made smaller by the silence that followed.

Jake smiled. "Only to Carl's plans. Reason number sixty-eight why you're not going to hear a lot of sweet talk about me from Carl or anyone else around here.''

"I don't understand.''

He shrugged and smiled. Being that she was Carl's fiancée, she probably wouldn't find Jake's opposition—or Carl's continual displeasure about it—as amusing as he did. "I don't think it would be all that interesting to you.'' He clapped his hands together. "Suffice it to say, I don't often agree with my family's business practices.''

"I'm interested," Joleen said, with a penetrating gaze that he couldn't ignore. "What do you mean?"

He met her eyes and something in him responded. Okay, he'd tell her if she really wanted to know. Maybe it would give her a clue about the man she was planning to marry. "There's a board meeting of Landon Industries on the fifteenth. We're voting on the takeover of a small, struggling company whose mortgage we own. Carl wants the takeover and I'm doing all I can to stop it."

"Why?"

He thought for a moment. "Because I'll be damned if I'm going to let Mr. Potter take over George Bailey's bank." He hesitated. Maybe she hadn't seen *It's a Wonderful Life*. "In other words, I don't want our big corporation to eat up small mom-and-pop organizations, because once that starts happening you can't stop it."

"I got it the first time." She smiled and it was beguiling. "We have television in Alvira, believe it or not, and I've seen the movie. And for what it's worth I agree with you. People lose a lot more than their livelihoods that way, they lose their self-worth and their self-respect. Towns lose their sense of community when small shops are depersonalized by large chains. I'm glad you're voting against it."

Jake regarded her in surprise for a moment. He was certain Carl didn't know about this side of Joleen, and he was equally certain he would be horrified if he did know. Some sort of alarm bell went off in his chest. "I appreciate it," he said. He wasn't used to expressing either appreciation or concern, and his voice came out awkward. "But you might want to watch who you say that to."

Joleen held his gaze for a long minute, and this time she didn't ask what he meant.

After she'd wasted as much time as she could unpacking, arranging and rearranging her clothes, Joleen finally acknowledged to herself that it was time to meet Jake's—and Carl's—mother.

She wasn't sure why she felt so hesitant. She'd wanted a big family all her life, and ever since her mother had passed away that need had become even more intense despite her close friendship with Marge. Now Carl was handing it to her on a solid silver platter. *Mother will help you with anything you need,* he'd told her. Joleen took a deep, satisfied breath and smiled. There was nothing to worry about. Surely Carl's mother would be as kind to her as he was. After all, she'd raised him.

With renewed confidence, Joleen picked up the phone to dial the housekeeper so she could make an appointment—or whatever it was they did around here—to see Mrs. Landon.

"Yes?" a voice asked sharply on the other line.

Joleen cleared her throat. "Yes, I wanted an appointment to see Mrs. Landon, can you tell me what I should do?"

"Who is this?" the voice was definitely impatient.

Joleen glanced at the receiver, then returned it to her ear and said, a little louder, "This is Joleen Wheeler. I'm staying…here…for a while." Suddenly she was all too aware that no matter what she said it sounded silly. "I'm Carl's—" She didn't know how to finish the sentence. Fortunately the woman on the phone did.

"Oh, Joleen, of course. Do come right up."

"Um, shouldn't I call Mrs. Landon first, or—"

"*This* is Virginia Landon speaking, dear." The voice was cultivated but had a razor-sharp edge. "You just rang my room."

Humiliation curled in the pit of Joleen's stomach. "Oh! I'm terribly sorry, I was trying to call the housekeeper."

"That is extension zero. Never mind, though, come right up. I'll be expecting you." Without any further instruction or even a goodbye, Virginia Landon hung up the phone.

Slowly Joleen lowered the receiver to the cradle. Trepidation crept across her skin, and she felt her palms break out into a clammy cold sweat. She was beginning to get the feeling that meeting Carl's mother was going to be more difficult than she'd anticipated.

Joleen took her time going through the hall to the staircase. Several times she stopped to pick up one of the *objets d'art* that were displayed on tables and shelves along the way. She also stopped at a small group of portraits and wondered if the incongruous mix was of Landon relatives or Virginia's relatives, or both. With the task that lay ahead she would gladly have stood and contemplated the point for several hours, but a voice inside told her to go on and get it over with.

Joleen mounted the stairs, wondering how she was

going to know which room belonged to Mrs. Landon. She hadn't dared call back to ask, but she also didn't want to take a chance on trying the maid again, for fear that she would get the wrong extension.

And she definitely didn't want to call Jake. He already thought she was painfully unsophisticated; she didn't want to reinforce that idea by asking how to find his mother in the great big house.

She started up the stairs, her pace set by a distant banging somewhere on the upper floor. With every step she took she was less certain that she could pull this off without making a complete fool of herself. What if she went to the wrong room? What if she went to the right room but it was the wrong time?

It was obvious which was the right room when she got to the top of the stairs because the scent of Guerlain's Shalimar trailed right to the door. Joleen knew Shalimar because the one luxury Marge afforded herself was an inexpensive imitation of the scent, which she only wore at Christmas time. The scent grew stronger with every step Joleen took toward the door, and she noticed it was similar to Marge's scent but somehow more subtle. A little more spicy and a little less sweet. Virginia Landon didn't use an imitation, Joleen was certain.

When she got to the bedroom door, she stopped to collect her courage. Virginia Landon lay back on a chaise longue that looked like something out of a 1930s movie, gazing at the television. Her auburn hair—a shade too bright—was pulled back severely and seemed to be pulling her red lips into a thin, mean line.

"You must be Joleen," Virginia called, placing a strange emphasis on *"leen."* She smiled but her eyes didn't change. "Do come in."

Her speech sounded affected to Joleen's ear, but Joleen figured that was because she'd been around roughnecks in Alvira for too long. She followed the sweep of the woman's hand like a puppet on an invisible string and sat down in the hard wooden chair Virginia indicated, even though there was a more comfortable looking cushioned wingback chair off to the side.

"So you want to marry my Carl," Virginia drawled, delicately pushing a button on the remote control. Sally Jessy Raphael snapped out of sight.

"I—I—we've talked about it," Joleen said, wondering what could have been on a daytime talk show that might interest a society queen like Virginia Landon.

"Just...talked about it?"

Joleen nodded. "Nothing's been decided for sure." *With any certainty,* she corrected herself mentally. *Talk like them.*

Virginia raised a penciled brow. "No? It was my impression that it was definite. Ah, well." The line of her mouth drew up slightly at the corners. The banging hammer resumed, and Virginia's mouth went straight again as she called toward the wall, "Jake, darling, could you stop that for a bit?" There was no answer, but she seemed satisfied with her effort and turned back to Joleen. "Carl tells me you'll be going to the One Mile Garden Club's opening tomorrow in his stead."

"Yes, he's asked me to."

Her eye swept down Joleen briefly. "I've taken the liberty of having some things sent for you. They should be here anytime now. I do hope you don't find that too presumptuous."

"It's fine," Joleen said, then took a deep breath to calm her frazzled nerves.

The hammering began again, and Virginia rolled her eyes heavenward and cried, "Jake Landon, will you *please* stop that hammering?"

A momentary silence followed, during which Joleen wondered what they were waiting for. Finally Virginia looked back at her.

"Unfortunately the staff is on vacation this month, as I'd planned to be in the south of France myself. The house needs some repairs and my younger son refuses to call a contractor for anything he feels he can do himself, so it's been absolute mayhem."

She shook her head and Joleen resisted the urge to do the same.

"What did you want?" Jake said to Virginia from the doorway.

"I wanted you to stop that infernal hammering, which you have." She extended her hand, gesturing him in, but he didn't move. "Joleen and I were just having a little chat about her future with Carl."

Jake did enter then. "Were you?" he asked, looking not at his mother but at Joleen.

"Actually we were talking about the park project I'm going to visit tomorrow," Joleen corrected.

"Yes." Virginia's voice dripped with honey.

"And I was trying to express to the dear girl how *no one* would be a better choice for the occasion."

Jake frowned and shifted one step closer to Joleen. "Yes, I'm sure Joleen will do a great job. Better than Carl could, no doubt."

Virginia frowned and sighed. "It breaks my heart the way you and your brother bicker."

"We don't bicker," he said to Joleen. He didn't look the least bit concerned about his mother's distress. "I'm not even sure *how* to bicker."

"Oh, I can't believe that," Joleen said quietly.

He smiled but his face flushed a little. "I was only kidding."

"Me too."

Their eyes held for a moment, then the corners of his eyes crinkled with just the merest hint of a smile. He inclined his head so slightly she might have missed it, then turned back to his mother.

"I think Joleen is perfect for the job." He tossed the hammer from one hand to the other. "Do you need anything else or can I get back to work?"

"Are you available tomorrow?"

"You know I'm available until the board meeting."

"Good. Then you won't mind taking Joleen to the park affair."

"I wouldn't," he drawled, "except that she's a grown woman, fully capable of getting herself around without a baby-sitter."

Virginia looked taken aback, a look she'd perfected over long years. "Darling, no one suggested the girl needed a baby-sitter, as you put it."

The girl. Virginia Landon was no longer even making eye contact with Joleen, she was simply talking about her as if she was an object to be moved from point A to point B.

"However," Virginia continued. "She *could* use a bit of supervision on her first official duties."

Jake turned to Joleen. "She doesn't mean that the way it sounds."

Joleen's face, which was already warm, went hot, then cold. "I—I'm sure if you just tell me where to go—"

"Nonsense, this will also show some family solidarity." She leveled her eyes on Jake. "Something that's been sadly lacking around here lately. Besides, he's available tomorrow, he just said so himself." Once again Virginia gave that smile that didn't quite reach her eyes.

Again Jake took a step closer to Joleen and she relaxed slightly as he inadvertently created a shield between his mother and her. Joleen knew Virginia was trying to use her as a pawn in some game between them—was Jake purposely trying to protect her? The comfort of his warmth and his scent wrapped around Joleen like a blanket.

Only then did she put the pieces together and realize that if Jake was on the side of "George Bailey" in a family squabble with Carl and Virginia, that must mean that Carl was... No, she couldn't believe that Carl wanted to railroad small businesspeople. His whole platform was based on opportunity for the little guy...wasn't it?

"I'll be glad to help out *if* Joleen wants my help," Jake said to Virginia.

Virginia sighed loudly. "Would that we were all so lucky."

His body went tense. "This is not the time for *that* conversation."

His mother ignored him. "You're more willing to help a stranger than family." She shook her head and pressed the back of her hand to her forehead. "It breaks my heart."

Joleen stood and took two steps backward, wondering if she could escape.

"Joleen is about to be family," Jake pointed out, making Joleen's stomach twist.

"Perhaps," Virginia agreed, looking down her nose at Joleen in the doorway. "Perhaps she is."

Jake straightened, and Joleen suddenly realized he could be very imposing. She'd hate to be on the wrong side of that.

"If you'll excuse me now," Joleen said, and swallowed. "I'd better go—" Go where? To the store? To the bathroom? To McDonald's? Home? She felt various levels of need to do all three. "I'd better go."

"Come back in an hour, dear, the clothes should be here by then."

"All right." Joleen stopped and turned back. "Mrs. Landon, please don't worry about how I'll do at the park dedication. I won't embarrass you or Carl."

The older woman looked surprised. "No, dear, I'm sure you won't."

Joleen smiled and turned to go. But as she left, she distinctly heard Virginia add to Jake, "Not that it matters that much. After all, the land will be sold in a couple of months, anyway, and the park will be no more."

When Joleen went back in an hour she was crippled by doubts about whether or not she should have called up first. She hadn't wanted to pester the woman, so she'd decided it best not to call. When she got to the doorway she tapped gently. "Mrs. Landon?"

"Yes, dear, come in."

Joleen walked in and saw that Virginia was on the telephone. "Yes, *I* do hate to say it but I believe it's true. Ah, well, one cannot control everything. Darling, I have to go now, there's a matter needing my immediate attention. Hmm? Yes, yes, I'll call you back." She kissed the air by the receiver and hung up. "Joleen, the packages have arrived. I'll have Jake bring them in for us."

"Oh, no, I can—"

"Jake!" It was amazing how shrill the woman's voice could be when she wasn't trying to modulate it.

Jake called something back and Virginia said, "We need your help right away."

Joleen frowned. He was going to think she was a complete ninny if she couldn't bring a few boxes of clothes in.

Jake appeared in the doorway. There was a faint

sheen of perspiration on his forehead. He was holding a leveler and a screwdriver. "Yep?"

"There are some boxes, Jake, would you mind—" Virginia fluttered her hand vaguely in the direction of the door.

"Playing Ping-Pong?"

Her eyes narrowed. "I'm asking you to get those boxes from the hall."

"Boxes in the hall. Right." With a short look at his mother and a longer one at Joleen, he stepped into the hall and came back with two long, brown boxes. He set them down by the chaise longue and said, "I'm going to try and get back to work now."

"No, no, darling, you must open the boxes. They're taped quite securely. I don't want to break my nails, and I see Joleen has very short ones." She looked pointedly at Joleen's hands.

Joleen glanced down at her short nails and thought for the millionth time what a bad nervous habit biting them was. She slipped them behind her back and looked at the boxes, instead of at Jake or Virginia.

"I have short nails, too, Mother," Jake said sharply. "It looks like you're best equipped to get the tape off."

"You have those things, those little knives."

"So do you," he muttered, digging in his pocket and producing a small Swiss army knife. "Honestly, Mother, I don't know how you get along without me here. I'm amazed there aren't boxes piled to the ceiling."

"Somehow we muddle through. But at the moment, with these extenuating circumstances..." She gestured toward her foot, which Joleen now saw was propped up with her toe wrapped in a lacy piece of fabric. "I really do need your help now and then."

"Hmm." With one swift movement, he ripped through the tape on each box and flipped the knife shut. "Okay. Now, if there's nothing else..." He started to leave.

"We could use a man's opinion," Virginia called behind him.

Joleen withered in embarrassment.

"You don't want my opinion," he answered, without stopping or turning around.

When he was gone, Virginia looked back to Joleen. "Mind you, I had to go by Carl's description of you to guess the size. Let's try that bigger box first. Take a few things out."

Joleen moved toward the box, wishing with every small step that she would disappear. When she got to the box and reached in, she couldn't believe her eyes. "There must be some sort of mistake," she said, pulling what looked like a shiny turquoise tent out of the box.

"No mistake, dear, I thought that would suit your coloring and my goodness it does."

"But the size," Joleen said, looking for the tag. "It's a size eighteen," she said incredulously. Maybe she was a little chubby, but if she was a size eighteen at her height she'd practically be round.

"Size eighteen would be too—" the hesitation while Virginia apparently ruminated over this was hideous "—large?" she ventured, with a raised eyebrow.

"I wear a ten."

"A ten, my goodness. Carl didn't say… Check the other box, I think there are sizes twelve and fourteen. Maybe they can be taken in." She hesitated just long enough to humiliate Joleen further saying, "If they need to be."

With neither hope nor spine, Joleen reached into the box and pulled out the only size twelve there. She pulled it out enough to see that it was a black evening dress, low cut in the front and back and with a short, slitted skirt. She was laying it back in the box when Virginia said, "That one. Try that one on."

Joleen turned around. "That's an evening gown."

"Nonsense, it's perfect, it's *you!* Do try it on."

The blood drained from her face. "I don't know. I was thinking maybe a nice cotton suit, more along the lines of Jackie Kennedy." *Not Madonna.*

Virginia laughed but it wasn't a kind sound. "Jackie Kennedy was quite a different type. I think I have a sense of your style. Just try it on, dear."

There was no saying "no" to this woman, so Joleen didn't even try. She went into the bathroom Virginia had indicated and closed the door behind her.

What was going on? Why did Carl's mother make her so uncomfortable? Immediately Joleen felt guilty for her thoughts. Virginia Landon was just trying to help her, and here Joleen was wishing she'd just go away and leave her alone. It was unforgivable.

She slipped out of her clothes and put on the dress Virginia had picked out. When she stood in front of the mirror she was shocked at how low the front dipped and how high the slit went. She felt naked. It would have been more comfortable to go out in public in a bikini, and Joleen wasn't planning on wearing one of *those* any time soon.

"How are you doing in there?" Virginia called.

"Um... I'm not sure this is really...suitable," Joleen returned. "In fact—"

"Let's see, come on out here."

"Okay. Just a moment." Joleen looked back at the mirror, trying to find some way to make the dress a little more modest. She barely registered the sound of voices murmuring outside the door until she stepped back into the room and saw not only Virginia but Jake gaping at her.

Virginia looked ecstatic. "It's exactly as I envisioned it. Jake, darling, isn't it perfect?"

"Perfect." He met Joleen's eyes and smiled. She felt, at that moment, that she had an ally. He looked back at his mother. "For someone else. Joleen doesn't look all that comfortable in it."

Something about the way he *didn't* look at her made Joleen all the more aware of her exposed flesh.

"What woman is comfortable with her own beauty?" Virginia mused. "Come now, no need for false modesty here, dear. You want the press to take notice of you and fast. This will do it. Believe me, it's *not* going to hurt Carl one bit to have those men appreciating you."

"So the wainscotting in the blue room," Jake said. "On or off?"

"On."

"Okay." Jake turned to go, tossing his screwdriver from one hand to the other as he left.

"Jake!"

He stopped.

"Perhaps you could at least tell Joleen how attractive she looks in her dress."

He inclined his head slightly and met Joleen's eyes, with a smile in his. "You're very attractive. Let me know if you need a ride to the store later. I can make the time, under the circumstances."

"Thanks," Joleen said in what sounded to her like a small voice. Then to Virginia she said, "It's a bit chilly in here so I think I'll just go back and change..." She gestured toward the bathroom, then turned and rushed in.

"It's just right," Virginia said, but Joleen wasn't sure if she meant the temperature or the dress. "I'm so pleased. Carl would be so surprised to see how easily we've taken care of things."

This time when Joleen looked in the mirror, she thought about how she might be able to make the dress less revealing, while still satisfying Virginia's insistence that it was *perfect*. She could put on a shawl, she decided, and opaque black hose. But was it really appropriate for a daytime event? Her instincts said no. But Virginia knew more about this sort of thing. Joleen had to remind herself of that.

If Virginia thought this dress would help draw some sort of beneficial attention to Carl's cause, then Joleen would wear it.

No matter how oogie it made her feel.

When Joleen came out she had decided to hurry

to the store before it closed so she could try and find some accessories to go with the dress. But it wouldn't be Neiman-Marcus—her budget wouldn't allow it. She'd have to find a Target or Wal-Mart. And she'd have to ask someone other than Virginia Landon where they might be.

"I'm thrilled we found such a suitable dress for you," Virginia said. "What a coup. But I suppose you'll be wanting to find more new clothes," she raked her gaze across Joleen, "as soon as possible. So I've set up an account for you at Neiman's."

"That's very generous of you, but—"

"Anything for my Carl. You'll also need to get an evening gown for the Governor's Ball this weekend. I've cut some pictures from a magazine to help guide your shopping."

Joleen froze. "Governor's Ball?"

"Yes." Virginia's gaze was cool, but the single word turned up like a question, clearly saying *and do you have a problem with that?* They probably all thought she was a terrible complainer, always hesitating to do her "duty" for the cause. "Here are the pictures." She handed Joleen a small pile of magazine clippings that looked like they came from a lingerie catalog.

"I'm sorry," Joleen said. "I don't know anything about the ball. But I'm sure Carl can fill me in and help me find something appropriate if we're going."

The look Virginia gave Joleen was decidedly condescending. "Carl has asked that I help you find something, so that he doesn't have to trouble himself with such incidentals."

"Oh. I see."

Madge used to joke about having "foot-in-mouth disease," now Joleen knew exactly what that felt like. She scanned her mind for the polite thing to say, something Katherine Hepburn might have said in *The Philadelphia Story*...but her mind was blank. Somewhere, somehow, she'd said or done the wrong thing, because Virginia Landon clearly didn't think much of her.

Well, Joleen was just going to have to change Virginia's mind. She was going to have to change all their minds.

Chapter Five

"I'm really sorry she made you do this," Joleen said as they parked Jake's car on a busy downtown street. Guilt gnawed away at her insides like a termite. "I'm sure you had better things to do than chauffeur me."

Jake put up his hand as he got out of the car. "Wait a minute—sorry *who* made me do *what?*"

"Your mother." She splayed her arms. "I'm sorry she made you bring me here today. Really, I can get back on my own. You just go on home."

"My mother hasn't *made* me do anything since I was ten years old." Joleen turned to look at him and he laughed. "All right, maybe twelve. But it's been years. I'm here because I want to help you."

Joleen's heart tripped, but she kept her eyes on the sidewalk in front of her. "You want to help me even though I'm helping Carl's campaign?" The hem of the black dress Virginia had picked for the occasion rode up and she pulled it at the hips and tried to tug it down. It was impossible to do casually.

"It's a conundrum, that's for sure." Jake stopped and took her arm, turning her gently to face him. "But if you're determined to go through with this—this *relationship* with Carl, I feel I should help you wherever I can."

There it was again, that implication that she was making a big mistake and he knew it. Joleen frowned. "With all due respect, I'm not sure Carl would consider that kind of statement to be helpful. It sounds like you don't think I *should* marry him."

"You said it." He shrugged. "So much for detachment, but at least I'm leaving soon."

"Detachment?" She tried to pull the low-cut V-neck up some. "What do you mean?"

His face warmed by one shade of red. "It's none of my business." He started walking again. "But if you're asking my opinion…"

"Okay, I am." She stopped.

He turned to look at her. They stood on a crowded intersection in one of the less-affluent parts of town. An early model dark blue sedan whizzed by and the driver whooped it up behind his tinted windows as he passed Joleen.

"I think you're trying real hard to be something you're not," Jake said. "All to please that sonofabitch Carl, who couldn't even be bothered to be here."

Joleen's breath caught in her throat. She'd expected blunt, but not *that* blunt! "I'm not all that different from you," she said defensively. "You make it sound like I'm a whole different species. I'm not a cat pretending to be a dog."

He studied her face for a moment. "That's not what I'm talking about."

"Then what *are* you talking about?"

"This dress. Is this you? Is this comfortable?"

"Clothes? You're talking about *clothes?*"

"Not just clothes." The light turned green and they walked across the street. "But you've got to admit, you never would have picked this out for yourself. As soon as Virginia told you this was a good choice, though, you agreed."

"I never agreed that this was a *good* choice." She certainly hadn't agreed. To her it seemed far too revealing, especially for a daytime event. Joleen bit her lower lip, then said, "Your mother thought it was and since she knows more about this kind of thing than I do it just made sense for me to—" what was the phrase? "—defer to her knowledge."

He snorted. "Your common sense can tell you a lot more about what's right than my mother can. Or will," he added under his breath.

Joleen wanted to agree, but her logical mind told her he was wrong. Her logical mind told her that small town instincts meant nothing in the big city. There was no way she could outdo the matriarch of the Landon family; she didn't have a clue about the protocol or the etiquette points that became so important when one was wealthy. "That's easy for you to say."

He gave a dry laugh, and Joleen caught the glint

of his blue eyes looking at her. "No, believe me, it's not."

"But you've been doing this all your life, haven't you?"

"Living a lie? You bet I have." He shoved his hands into his pockets. "But I've decided to stop. How about you?"

She took a deep breath and noticed it shuddered. "I'm not living a lie."

"In other words, you enjoy going to this sort of thing? This political campaign point?"

"I don't know. I've never done it before."

"Okay, then, we'll see." He stopped and waved his hand in front of them to indicate a verdant city park, encompassing a block that swarmed with news media and citizens. Some were dressed in obviously expensive clothes: tropical-weight wool suits, tailored dresses, gleaming leather shoes. Others wore the uniform of the streets: torn, baggy jeans, dirty T-shirts, old military and sports jackets, and worn-out sneakers.

But some of those people, Joleen could tell, were the wealthy benefactors of the park project, working their hands into blisters with the shiny new shovels and garden equipment. She wondered just how many of them would be working on the project if it weren't so highly publicized, then chastised herself for even having the thought.

A red-headed woman in a T-shirt and dirt-stained jeans approached them. "Joleen Wheeler?" She wiped her hand on her jeans and extended it to Joleen. "I'm Nancy Migglin, one of the heads of this

Green and Clean project. I'm so glad you could make it."

Joleen took the woman's hand and shook it. The V-neck of her dress shifted as she did, and she immediately pulled her hand back to adjust it. "Pleased to meet you." She pushed her bra strap back under her dress then looked up at Nancy and smiled briefly.

Nancy's eyes flicked over to Jake. "How ya doing, Jake? Long time, no see."

He nodded and smiled a smile that Joleen couldn't interpret. She suddenly felt uncomfortable.

Nancy turned back to Joleen. "So." She clapped her hands together. "Would you like the grand tour?"

Jake hung back as Nancy took Joleen across the grassy city block, pointing out the flower garden, the vegetable garden and the magnificent herb garden in the center. She talked about how important the project was to the children, and how much they'd already gotten out of it. The statistics on decreasing crime were not large, but they were promising.

"Next year we hope to have enough vegetables to join the Saturday farmer's market uptown throughout the summer."

Joleen hesitated. *Next year?* Nancy must have meant *this* year.

Before she could figure out how to ask, they reached Jake again and Nancy said to Joleen, "Look, I can't tell you how great it is that your husband is letting us use this land. I hope it prospers for years and years."

There it was again. Joleen frowned, not bothering

to correct Nancy on her marital status. "You mean...here?"

Nancy laughed. "Well, yes, Mr. Landon has promised us the use of the land indefinitely. 'As long as it's his,' he said. And I don't think Carl Landon is going anywhere, do you?" She smiled brightly.

Joleen was puzzled. "But I thought... No, *he's* not going anywhere. But didn't someone else buy the land?" Then it occurred to her. "Oh, you mean the *new* owners are letting you keep the park, too."

Nancy's eyes narrowed. "What?" The single word was a shard of glass that cut right through what was left of Joleen's self-confidence.

"The land has been sold—" Joleen turned to Jake "—hasn't it?"

He shrugged. "I stay out of the family business." He lowered his chin and looked at her in an I-tried-to-warn-you way.

Joleen turned back to a befuddled Nancy. "I don't really know the details but I'll try to find out."

"Yeah," Nancy said in a hollow voice. "Thanks, but that's not going to do much good." She looked back at the park and shook her head.

"Have you thought about trying to use designated parkland?" Joleen asked. "That way there would be no risk of ever losing the property—" she looked behind Nancy at the colorful garden "—and all your hard work."

Nancy's face had gone pale. "The problem is that there is no parkland." Her voice was hardening as she spoke, her anger crystallizing. "That's why Mr. Landon's offer seemed such a godsend."

"But there *is* city property that's not being used. Like over on the west side, what's the name of that place?" She concentrated. She'd just passed it on her way to Neiman-Marcus the other day and made a mental note of it. "I can't remember, but it's an old overgrown courtyard. I'll bet the city would just love to have someone come along and maintain it."

"You mean until Carl Landon takes office and turns it into an oil rig, don't you?" Nancy's eyes were cold. Joleen shivered, feeling with shock the damning association with Carl's actions.

Suddenly the feeling of having said way too much washed over her, and she was sure her own face went pale. "Ms. Migglin, please don't take what I said too seriously until we find out the facts. I may be wrong about the sale of the land." *But I don't think so.*

"Maybe the press can find out, and faster than you or I could." Nancy turned to the crowd. "Hey! We've got some news over here!"

"Oh, no, *please,*" Joleen said. "Please let me find out first. If I'm wrong, this could cause an awful lot of trouble for Carl." Not that Nancy had any concern for that at this moment, but there was another consideration. "Not to mention heartache for the kids and the rest of your team."

A team of reporters was rushing over.

"*Please,*" Joleen begged.

"Nance," Jake interjected. "You know how I feel about this sort of thing, but Joleen's right. If these facts are mixed up, this could look really bad for everyone."

Nancy appeared to consider this, then nodded

slowly. When the reporters and newsmen arrived and asked what the excitement was, Nancy said, "This is Mr. Landon's wife—"

"Fiancée," Jake corrected.

"Actually," Joleen started, "we're just—"

But her voice was lost in the roar of questions to Jake.

"How long have you been engaged, Mr. Landon?"

"Where did you meet?"

Someone, somewhere, said to call *People Weekly*.

And to Joleen, "What's it like to be engaged to the man *Texas Monthly* voted this year's most eligible bachelor?"

"Jake, you old sonofagun!"

"I—"

Jake stepped slightly closer to her and said, "Joleen is engaged to my brother, Carl Landon, not to me." He turned and looked at her for a long moment. His gaze made her vaguely uncomfortable, and she realized it was because her heart was pounding.

When he turned back to the madding crowd he added, simply, "My brother is a very lucky man."

Either no one had warned Joleen to remain politically correct—as defined by Carl—or she'd flat-out disregarded the instruction, Jake thought as he worked alone in the barn, getting ready to wrap a brood mare's legs. It was hard to believe that neither Carl nor Virginia had told her to keep her mouth shut, but neither could he believe that a shy, polite-as-a-child girl like Joleen would deliberately sabotage Carl's campaign.

That left only one option: Carl and Virginia had just assumed she was too stupid to say something dangerous.

He went to the tack room for bandages and laughed to himself. Oh, Joleen was dangerous all right. She was the worst kind of dangerous to the Landon family: she was honest. He might have felt sorry for her, for the misery she was letting herself in for by marrying Carl, but Jake was a little too pleased at the thought of having an ally in the family.

The mare whinnied restlessly.

"I know it," Jake said, opening the stall door and running a hand along the bay mare's sleek neck and across her withers. "You're ready to get out of here." He sighed and continued to stroke her. "So am I, old girl, so am I."

"Hello?" a voice called from the barn entrance. "Is anyone here?"

Joleen. Jake straightened and ran a hand through his hair to straighten it. "Back here." He reached over and unlatched the door just as Joleen walked up.

"What can I do for you?" he asked, trying to ignore the stupid somersault his heart did.

"Actually, I was just...wandering. Thinking."

"About today?"

She nodded and walked over to the stall next to him. "Today, yesterday, tomorrow." She stopped and leaned over the stall door. "What's her name?" she asked, peering in at the mare.

"This is Trouble." Joleen turned and looked at him, and he laughed. "The horse, her name is Trouble. Best brood mare I've got. Direct line descendent of Secretariat, the greatest racehorse that ever lived, in my opinion." He went into the stall.

"I remember." Joleen nodded. "Won the Triple Crown in the early seventies."

He nodded. "Nineteen seventy-three. I didn't know you were a racing fan." Though he was starting to realize there were a lot of things about Joleen that he found surprising. He squatted by one of the mare's front legs and began to carefully wind the fabric bandage around her fetlock.

"I won a quarter on that race. My uncle was a real fanatic, but he had the idea Secretariat couldn't pull it off." She laughed. "He was usually wrong about people, too."

"At least you profited." They were talking about nothing, but in a deliberate way. He braced his hand on the horse's chest and pulled the bandage tight.

Joleen trailed her finger lightly along the horse's shoulder. Jake shivered, imagining the touch on his own skin. It had been a long time. It must have been or he never would have associated that kind of thought with Joleen.

"She looks restless." Joleen smiled. "Like she wants to get out of here and run free."

"She does. But there's a stallion out there who can't be contained and I don't want him getting to her." He clapped his hand against the horse's shoulder and moved to her other front leg. "Got to keep the ol' gene pool pure."

Joleen laughed. "We girls can't be trusted to know what's good for us, can we?"

"Hell, she wouldn't even know what hit her."

"I know that feeling."

Jake looked at Joleen's profile, so serious and concerned about the horse's welfare. She continued to stroke the mare and he watched, thinking a person's compassion for animals was a really good indicator of character.

It came as no surprise that Joleen was compassionate with animals.

"You didn't do anything wrong, you know," he said, after a few minutes. He tried to see her face but she continued looking at the horse. He started wrapping again, concentrating his vision on the green bandage. "I mean today, at the park."

She drew in a long breath. "I did something terribly wrong," she said, continuing to look straight ahead. "I might have damaged Carl's reputation."

"If anyone damaged Carl's reputation it was Carl," he told her, keeping his eyes on his work.

"Maybe."

He tucked the end of the bandage in and glanced at her. "Definitely." He stood and opened the door to come out.

She dropped her arm and turned to face Jake as he moved before her. "But that doesn't mean I should be chattering away like that. I really put my foot in it." She looked at him with liquid blue eyes and, without thinking, he stepped toward her.

At the last second, realizing it was a mistake, he shifted his weight and leaned against the stall door.

"Have you ever thought that maybe you'd be happier living a life where you didn't have to worry about 'putting your foot in it'?" He reached over and unlatched the door. He knew he should stop both moving and speaking but he couldn't.

"I'm happy with my life," she said softly, looking up at him.

He took a small step toward her, and she stood her ground. "Are you really?" he asked. He'd been holding a rolled bandage and he set it down on an overturned water bucket.

"Really," she answered, too quickly. Her arms crossed over her chest. "I have more hope for the future than I've ever had in my life." As soon as the words were out she looked down, and Jake saw her close her eyes for a moment. She was embarrassed. He wished she wasn't.

"What, exactly, do you hope for the future?" he asked quietly, soothingly, as though to keep the mare, not Joleen, from shying at the sound of his voice.

She frowned, as if she wasn't sure whether he was being sarcastic or not. "I hope to make something of myself, and to make a difference in people's lives, maybe help sick children."

"You can do that anywhere."

She gave a derisive snort. "I hope to do something more important than wait tables in some greasy spoon in a small town where nothing happens and nothing matters."

"You happened there," Jake said. "You matter." Her gaze flew to him, wide-eyed, and he added quickly, "I admire the fact that you want to help people. Most people don't care that much about anyone else."

She stroked the horse's flank. "I'm nothing special."

Jake's heart twisted but he didn't know what to say that wouldn't become an "am not" "are too" argument so he simply said, "I'm sure there are a lot of people who would disagree with that."

She looked at him with such softness in her eyes that he felt his throat constrict. "You're a nice guy, Jake Landon. More people should know that."

"Only a few people's opinions matter to me."

She nodded. "I'm sure mine isn't one of them, but I had to say it, anyway."

He wanted to tell her that her opinion did matter. Instead he shrugged and turned his attention back to the mare.

"Does she run anymore?" Joleen asked, reaching out to stroke the horse's neck again.

"Nah, she's in the business of making foals now," Jake said, patting the horse's neck.

Joleen's hand brushed against Jake's on the horse's coat and she drew it back fast.

He made a point of looking at his watch. "I've got an appointment soon, was there anything in particular that you needed?"

"No, thanks." She smiled briefly.

She was so pretty, he thought.

"I guess I really just wanted to thank you for helping out today," she finished.

Truth was, he'd enjoyed it. He shouldn't have. "Just doing my duty."

"Oh. Well. Thanks, anyway."

He nodded.

She started to walk away, then stopped. "I know you and your mother don't think I'm...right...for your family, but I'm really going to do my best for Carl."

Like the jerk deserved it. "I'm sure you will."

"Maybe someday you'll even like me," she added, almost under her breath but loud enough for him to hear.

Jake felt like he'd been sucker-punched right in the gut. "Joleen, where did you get the idea that I don't like you?"

"It's been obvious," she answered, with more deference than that belief should have merited. "Your asking what a girl like me is doing with Carl, and telling me what a fraud I am for trying to fit in with your family."

"I never said you were a fraud."

"Yes, you did. You just didn't use that word."

"I said you were trying to be something that you're not. That's not necessarily a fraud. I think you're just a nice girl with a pretty dream that doesn't quite meet with reality. At least not Carl's reality."

"So I'm a fool."

"No." He stopped and asked himself if that *was* what he meant. But it wasn't. He didn't believe she was a fool for a minute. "I think you're a romantic."

She'd grown very still. "That sounds like a euphemism for a fool."

He shook his head. "Look, you come from a small town where everyone knows each other and nothing much happens. A lot of girls in that situation get their ideas about love and marriage from the movies and books. All I'm saying is that life isn't always like that."

"Oh, really?" Her eyes narrowed. "You mean I'm not going to fall asleep for a hundred years and be awakened by my true love's kiss? That's not going to happen?" Her voice had grown decidedly sharp.

What the hell had he done? He'd only tried to help. "I don't know." He reached over the stall door, took Trouble's nearly empty water bucket and dumped it on the cement floor. "How long have you been asleep so far?"

She made a sound of incredulity and he took the bucket to the water spigot to avoid meeting her eyes.

"For your information, not everyone who grows up outside the big city thinks beans are a good trade for a cow or that fairy godmothers take care when the going gets tough."

"Right." He jerked the water pump down. "Some of you think Prince Charming takes care instead."

"*Most* of us take care of ourselves."

"Of course. That's why you're trying so hard to be the princess of Carl's dreams...no matter what you have to give up." He hauled the heavy bucket back over the stall door, sloshing water at their feet, and hooked it on.

"I'm not giving up anything!"

"You're giving up yourself."

Her face grew bright red. "Look who's talking—the guy who gave up a family inheritance, money that could have been used to help people, in order to act out the role of the rebellious black sheep of the family."

"I'm not acting out *any* role." He moved to the next stall and took the water bucket out. It was already full, but he dumped the contents in the straw and took it over to the water pump, just to keep busy. "I'm doing what's right for me."

"Well, I'm doing the same thing."

He pulled the pump up and the water streamed out into the bucket. "You don't even *know* what's right for you!"

"How is it *you* can know what's best for *everyone* and *I* can't even know what's best for *me?*"

"Because *I* have experience and you don't." It sounded simple enough, and he meant it simply, but his heart was pounding with adrenaline.

She put her hands on her hips. "How do you know?"

He laughed, but it didn't sound as knowing as he'd wanted it to. "I know, believe me."

"Is that right?" She took a step toward him.

Somehow his heart rate increased. "How many times have you been engaged, Joleen?"

"Is that a measurement of experience?" Her voice got slightly softer. "Engagement? Maybe *you're* the one who's naive."

He looked down at her and smirked. "All right, now many times have you...been kissed?"

She tilted her chin up. "Kissed?" she asked, her voice dripping with unexpected seduction.

He took a quick breath. "Yeah, kissed."

"I didn't know men of the world like you thought about things as mundane as kissing."

"Darlin' when it's done right, it's anything but mundane. But maybe you wouldn't know that."

She raised an eyebrow. "And I suppose *you're* the man to show me."

She was playing with fire and gasoline was coursing through his veins. "Maybe I am."

She laughed. "I don't think you could show me anything I don't already know better."

His lips curled into half a smile. "Care to make a wager?"

"What does the winner get?"

"You."

"What does the loser get?"

"Me."

She wet her lips unconsciously. "Doesn't sound like much of a bet."

"Try me."

"I'm not a gambling woman."

"You won a quarter on Secretariat in 1973." He took another step closer to her. They were only about a foot apart. "What's changed?"

"The stakes, evidently." But she didn't back away.

"I understand why you're scared—"

"I'm not scared."

He regarded her with silence for a moment, then said, "You're scared. You're a little girl playing Cinderella, and you can't face the fact that not all men are princes and not all wolves are bad."

"Which are you?" she asked in a voice that nearly broke.

"Which do you want me to be?"

"It's none of my business." She turned away and tossed over her shoulder, "But I think we've determined who it is that's playing make-believe here."

He caught her arm and turned her back to face him. "Play with me."

Her sharp intake of breath aroused him. "I won't."

"You can't."

"It would be wrong."

"It would be great." He took one more step toward her, closing the gap between them. He reached out and trailed his finger down the side of her face, then down her throat. He stopped at her breast bone and returned his gaze to her eyes. "And educational."

Her nostrils flared slightly with her breath. "You're trying to goad me."

"I'm trying to *educate* you." He bent down and nuzzled her ear in a way that usually reduced women to liquid.

"I think you're looking for practice," she said. It was a good shot but he'd already seen her swallow nervously.

He moved his lips to her throat. "Is that what you call it?"

She put her hand up as if to stop him, but when his lips touched the hollow of her throat, she sighed and her hand stayed resting against his chest. "This doesn't do a thing for me. You're really looking pretty foolish right now."

He smiled against her neck. He could feel her rapid pulse against his mouth. He trailed his tongue across the spot, then said, "Does this do anything for you?"

"No."

He cradled the back of her head with his hands and ran his tongue lightly along her jawline and behind her ear. She tilted her head as he did, making the way easier for him.

"This?" he asked softly. That move *always* worked.

"No," she answered, with a waver in her voice.

He covered her mouth with his and dipped his tongue in against hers, taking her taste fully into his own mouth. Suddenly he wasn't sure who was in control, if anyone was.

In a move as sudden as his had been slow, Joleen raised her hands to cup his face and kissed him deeply. Her tongue worked masterfully against his, and the rhythm of her small kisses increased as his passion increased.

He clamped his arms around her and she moaned very lightly, very briefly, deepening her kisses still more. Her fingernails brushed lightly against his temples and worked their way down his scalp to the back of his neck, where she laced her hands behind his head and held him firmly against her mouth.

Then she moved one hand to his chest and ran a single fingernail down across his chest and his stomach, stopping short at the waistline of his jeans.

Then she went still, drawing the kiss out to a lingering finish. The wet sound of their lips parting was like a shock to his groin.

Then, as suddenly as she'd started, Joleen pulled back and looked him in the eye. "Still think I'm naive?" she asked, breathless.

His own breath came in short pants that mirrored hers. "Yes," he answered, then lowered his mouth onto hers again.

She pulled back. "We can't do this."

"We can."

"We shouldn't."

"We really should. Now." He tried to kiss her again but she stepped back.

"It was a mistake," she said. "You goaded me into it. Okay, we goaded each other." She swallowed, then swallowed again, knowing that, no matter what she said, she'd been as affected by him as he had been by her. "It didn't mean anything."

He didn't move toward her, though he wanted to. "Didn't it?"

She looked down. "No, it didn't. It was a childish game. We should both be ashamed of ourselves. I know I am."

He touched a finger to her chin. "Do we have to compete on that, too?"

She almost laughed, he could tell. "No."

"Good."

She met his eyes. "But you have to understand, that can never happen again."

"*I* have to understand that?"

She looked bemused by his question. "Well, yes."

"What about you?"

"What about me?"

He shifted his weight and wished there was something he could do with his hands other than let them dangle uselessly at his sides. The one thing that came to mind was clearly inappropriate. "I don't recall saying it would happen again," he said.

She lowered her brows and her blue eyes became mere slits. "Good."

"Good."

"Because it won't."

He gave a shake of the head. "That's fine by me."

She pursed her lips, then nodded. "Okay. We're clear. That was a mistake, we goaded each other into it, and it didn't mean a thing."

"Not a thing."

She hesitated, studying him, then added, "And it will never happen again."

"Right."

"Right." After another moment's hesitation, she said, "I'm going now."

Jake had already turned away and was fidgeting with the bit on a bridle that happened to be hanging by Trouble's stall. "See ya," he said, without turning around.

"'Bye." He heard her footsteps clop out of the barn onto the dirt outside and back again. "You know," she called again. "I'm really not going into this blindly."

He turned to face her, then looked down at her shoes. Or, more specifically, what she had stepped in on her way back into the barn. "You're not, huh?" Jake asked.

She followed his gaze down to her feet and made an exclamation of displeasure. "I meant my relationship with Carl," she said, trying to scrape the sullied side of her shoe against the pavement. "I'm not going into this relationship with Carl blindly."

"That's a good thing," he answered, keeping his eyes on her shoe. "I wish you both the best of luck."

"Thank you." Her foot stopped its frantic motion against the pavement and Jake looked into her eyes. "So...we've forgotten this little incident?" she asked.

He smiled, knowing she had no idea how his heart was pounding or his mind was reeling. "What incident?"

She smiled after a moment. "Right. No incident at all. I'm going in now."

"Better leave your shoes at the door."

She flashed him a look. "Thank you."

He nodded and turned back to the bridle, wondering what on earth he could even pretend to do to it until Joleen was out of sight. He fidgeted with the buckles until it seemed like enough time must have passed and he turned back to the barn opening. "You're welcome," he said softly at the figure making her way up to the main house. "Cinderella."

Chapter Six

Joleen felt ill at ease as she was getting ready for bed that night. Her conscience was nagging at her, insisting she wasn't cut out for this life. Just like Jake said.

But Jake would have said that to any girl who wasn't a debutante, she reasoned. He didn't think she was good enough. Of course, he would have argued that point, but Joleen got the message loud and clear. Either he didn't think she was good enough or he didn't think she was smart enough to step into the public eye as a Landon.

Either way it stank.

Joleen hesitated. Yes, it stank, but it was true. She sat heavily in the window seat near her bed. *Could* she learn to keep her mouth shut at some times and be charming and witty other times? Could she learn to tell the difference? Could she change herself at all, or did she even want to?

She straightened. Yes, she wanted to. The alternative was to rot in the diner in Alvira, going to night school until she was old enough to be brought in as a guest speaker "eyewitness" for history classes. *Joleen Wheeler, 97, discusses the history of the automobile and what it was like to ride in a car with wheels.*

She laughed at the idea. Maybe that was a little extreme, but still, she'd probably be over forty before she graduated at this rate. *After* that she could think about the rest of her life. She wanted a family, children. Even if she met another man and fell madly in love, did she really want to leave her children in day care while she worked all day, then leave them again at night so she could go to school? She didn't want to have children and then miss their childhood, but she also couldn't imagine giving up the dream of finishing college and doing something important with her life.

She leaned back. Carl didn't know about her dream. That hadn't occurred to her before. She'd told Jake, but not Carl. But then again, Jake had asked.

He'd asked what she wanted to do with her life, what was important to her, and she'd told him. Now she wasn't about to let his prejudiced contention that she shouldn't try to improve herself drive her away.

She looked out the window over the expanse of land that was the ranch. The moon was waxing, and was bright enough to illuminate the miles of field that stretched out to the horizon. Joleen thought it looked like a fairy-tale land, touched by silvery light, unmarred by man. Trees, horses and cattle dotted the landscape like small dark smudges on a clean sheet of paper.

The sky was deep purple, and far greater than the land it looked down upon. If the land was the place for fairy-tales, the sky was the place for fairies. Everywhere Joleen looked there were stars except to the right, where the city of Dallas lit the sky like the north star must have two thousand years ago.

Okay, maybe it wasn't Jake's prejudiced contention that was giving her pause. He was probably just trying to be nice; she was almost sure he thought he was doing her a favor. No, it was her own fear of failure. That kind of fear was useless. She refused to indulge it anymore. Everything had seemed so clear before she'd gotten here. She needed to get back to her old resolve. She was going to give this new life her best shot and nothing was going to stop her.

Having made the decision, Joleen felt immediately better. She pushed the window halfway open and leaned against the sill. A warm breeze touched her face and she sighed. She took a long breath and let it out with the remnants of tension from the day. It was peaceful, that was the word. In Alvira it was *quiet,* but here it seemed *peaceful.* The difference between the two was striking.

Her mother used to have an old record of Bing Crosby singing "Deep in the Heart of Texas" and the remembered voice came back to her now. She'd always wondered where that glorious Texas that Bing sang about was, and now she knew. Here. And the cowboys of those romantic old songs?

Jake.

That was an objective assessment, Joleen told herself, not **a** personal one. He emitted masculinity like a scent, but his unawareness of that fact was the thing that really pushed him over the edge. Carl was handsome, absolutely, but in a self-conscious sort of way. He seldom smiled when it wasn't for effect.

Funny, she'd never thought about that before.

But Jake smiled often and easily. Just like he frowned. If something struck him as wrong, he didn't look away or put a spin on it so he could ignore it. He spoke up. She liked that. She *admired* that.

She also liked the way he moved, the easy gait of his walk and the powerful suggestion of his stance. He was really good cowboy material, she decided. Just like something out of a book.

Joleen frowned. Why the heck couldn't she stop thinking about him? If she wasn't mulling over the things he'd said to her, she was mulling over the way he looked and the way he sounded and the way he smelled. And of course there was the kiss she'd been trying not to think of all day long. It had to stop. She had to concentrate on something else—anything else—even that song.

It was on the second mental chorus of "Deep in the Heart of Texas" that a light snapped on in the guest house, startling Joleen with its proximity—about a twenty-second walk. A moment earlier the little house had been so cloaked in darkness that she'd almost forgotten it was there. Now not only was it there, but so was Jake.

She saw him toss something down on a chair and walk into the kitchen. It was vaguely reminiscent of watching an old sitcom where the cheap film sets consisted of three rooms side by side which the characters moved about in. As he passed through the kitchen, he pulled his shirt off, revealing a torso more muscular than Joleen had realized. His skin was deeply tanned, and shadows dipped and curved, highlighting every muscular peak and valley. Beautiful, she thought.

Joleen tried to tell herself that this was an objective observation. Rather like one might have upon beholding Michelangelo's David for the first time. Maybe she should have been a casting agent or something. She'd never realized it before but she seemed to have a pretty good eye for physical appearances.

Carl, for example, would have made a good... She thought about that. Carl wasn't as easy as Jake. Jake she could see as a cowboy in faded jeans and chaps; a Greek god in a small drape of fabric; even as a matador in red and gold regalia. Hmm, maybe especially as a matador in red and gold regalia.

But Carl? Carl was a politician. He *looked* like a politician. He was perfect, she told herself, in a futile attempt at comfort. Carl was perfect just as he was.

Joleen turned her attention back to the house outside. Whether she should have been watching or not, she could see Jake perfectly.

He walked to the refrigerator and pulled it open lazily. He reached in and took a beer can, opening it as he kicked the door shut. He passed back through the kitchen and foyer again, and the front door opened. Joleen shrank back. This was shameful—she was *spying* on him.

He stepped out onto the porch and she heard the clop of his shoes against the wood. Joleen froze, wondering what to do. After a moment, she strained for one last glimpse, but he moved into the shadows of the porch and sat down on a rocker. She could hear the soft, slow creak as he moved back and forth. She saw the light move across his features then shroud him in mystery, again and again.

She had to look away.

She pushed off the windowsill and stood up, turning her attention to the room around her. The dim light from the back of the room suddenly seemed too bright, and she closed her eyes against it for a moment. When she opened them, it was less glaring. *That's what you get for spying,* she chided herself, *you get blinded.*

Not that spying was her greatest sin of the day. The one thought she'd been trying all day to avoid flooded into her mind like Noah's rain: the memory of Jake's kiss and how it had made her melt like wax in his arms. She recalled the fit of his mouth over hers. Every movement he'd made had reduced her resistance until she'd reached the point where she might have been powerless to stop. Her heart pounded wildly at the thought.

She'd done the right thing. She had, somehow, managed to stop it and to tell Jake it must never happen again. In her opinion, she'd even sounded as if she had conviction behind her words. But in her heart she knew if he'd pulled her back into his arms at that moment she would have let him. She may even have been glad.

No kiss she'd experienced in all her life had made her feel the way Jake's had. She'd felt like a cat, arching toward his touch, needing, wanting, *craving* at least one more moment of it. She let out a ragged sigh. It was like a hunger she hadn't known she'd felt but was now hard-pressed to forget.

But she would. She had to. It had been a mistake on both their parts. Whoever Jake had been thinking of in that moment, it probably wasn't Joleen any more than she'd been thinking of him. She'd been thinking of Carl, of course, thousands of miles away on some French coast.

Carl, she thought. If she'd ever needed him, she needed him now.

She ran her hands across her bare arms where gooseflesh had raised. How could she be chilly in the middle of July in Dallas? Maybe her nightgown was just too skimpy. She went to the closet to take out her robe, hesitating for a moment at the chest of drawers. The garish ring Carl had given her glittered brightly, giving her a strange shudder. Turning away from the ring, she hurried on to get the robe. Not that Jake would be watching her the way she'd been watching him, but she sure as heck didn't want to be accused of being an exhibitionist in front of her possible future brother-in-law.

Brother-in-law. That would make Carl her husband. She would be Carl's wife. Her mouth felt dry and she went to the bathroom for a cup of water. Why did the idea of being Carl's wife suddenly make her so uncomfortable? It hadn't exactly made her heart sing before, but it had seemed a pleasant possibility. Now she felt something more like dread.

She remembered her faux pas at the park opening. She'd made such a fool of herself that the idea of marrying Carl and perhaps repeating today's performance was horrifying. She would *have* to be more careful from now on.

Yes, that was all it was. That and the fact that she hadn't seen Carl in a few weeks. She missed him. It was such a curious phenomenon, this missing someone and having it feel like indifference. Oh well, it wasn't as though she'd ever been this close to a man before. More experienced women were probably used to all the guises their emotions took on.

Jake crunched his beer can in the distance, bringing Joleen's attention reeling back to him. She glanced out the window then quickly averted her eyes. Silly. He wasn't going to see her. Of course he wasn't watching her, he had no interest in her whatsoever—and why should he?

She secured the robe around her waist and went to the bathroom for another cup of water. Glancing in the mirror as she filled the paper cup she noticed how chunky she still looked around the center. In the movies, women put on their thin silk robes and looked trim and sexy. Joleen looked like a housewife in a bad spoof. All she was lacking was a pair of pink fluffy bunny slippers and curlers in her hair.

She pushed her hair out of her eyes and went back to the bedroom. She had to get over her self-consciousness. No one was watching, especially not

Jake. She picked up the book off the bedside table and flopped down on the bed to read. It wasn't until after she'd shrugged out of her robe that she realized her reading glasses were in her purse by the door and she had to get back up to retrieve them.

It occurred to her to close the blinds just in case the movement caught Jake's eye and he looked over to see her hefting around in her nightshirt. But that was stupid, she told herself, suppressing the chill that ran down her back as she hesitated at the window. All this speculation about Jake was stupid. Just like the tingling she felt all over her body as the warm wind touched her skin.

It had just been too long since she'd seen Carl.

Jake glanced out the window. Joleen's light was still on even though it was well past midnight. So she was a night owl, just like him. Somehow that fact didn't surprise him.

What was she doing? he wondered. What had she been doing all night? Hopefully she'd stopped beating herself up about telling Nancy Migglin how Carl was planning to sell the parkland. Jake shook his head. That was the most damnable thing about the way his family operated. Despite their shady deals and underhanded plays, somehow it was the honest guy who always ended up feeling like he'd done something wrong.

He pulled his shirt off over his head and threw it on a chair. God, he needed to get away from here. A movement in Joleen's window caught his eye but he resisted looking. He needed to get *far* away. He went to the kitchen and took a beer from the refrigerator, popping the top with one hand while he kicked the door shut. For just a split second he wished it was Carl his foot connected with.

Damn Carl for taking a nice girl and trying to make her into an unscrupulous spin doctor like himself. Joleen thought she'd done something heinous by telling the truth. It didn't even occur to her that Carl had done anything wrong. *Carl.* Man, he was so sick of thinking about Carl. He took a gulp of beer. How long would it take for Jake to finally learn, once and for all, that he couldn't fix everything Carl broke?

He went out to the front porch and inhaled the thick air. A movement near Joleen's window caught his eye again. This time he couldn't resist; he looked across. She was near the window, close enough for him to see that the long T-shirt she wore said NRBQ across it in faded lettering. He smiled. She had good taste in music. Then he laughed. What did his behind-the-times brother Carl think of that?

Joleen walked across the room, and Jake stopped in the doorway, letting his eyes trail down her shapely legs. Why not? He was a safe distance away; there was no chance of making her uneasy with his attention. Not that there was anything wrong with a man simply appreciating a woman's beauty. It wasn't like he attached any significance to it. She was just a pretty girl, with an incredible body and a walk that made his pants feel too tight. He drank. Nothing immoral about that.

Jake heaved his weight into the ancient wooden

rocker and took a long, cool pull of his beer. He had to get his mind off Joleen and onto something else.

This was some heat wave they were having. He raised the cold can to his forehead. Hell of a heat wave.

His eyes slipped back to her window. She pulled a thick terry cloth robe out of the closet and tied it at the waist. He could imagine what it would feel like to pull her into his arms and slowly untie the sash.

He couldn't help it, he thought of the kiss they'd shared earlier. He thought of the smell of her hair and the taste of her mouth. He thought of kissing her again. He'd kissed women before but he'd never felt an intense compulsion to do so like he had with Joleen.

Across the expanse of lawn and house, Joleen walked back across the room to the bathroom. Even the way she moved, barefoot and swathed in terry cloth, arrested Jake's imagination. Her movements seemed to say that she was complete, that she was self-sufficient...that she was a whole woman, with her own thoughts, opinions and experiences to share. All of that, Jake thought bitterly, *all* of it would be wasted on Carl.

A six-pack of beer sat on the porch by his feet. Jake couldn't remember how it had gotten there, but he knew he'd been meaning to take it in for a couple days now. At this moment, though, it seemed like good fortune. He reached down and took one of the warm cans from the plastic that held them. Still watching Joleen, he popped the top open. Foam exploded from the top of the can and ran down his hand and leg. It soaked right through the denim onto his thigh. He barely noticed. He just swiped his wet hand across his jeans and took a long pull of the warm liquid.

Joleen had gotten a cup of water. For a moment Jake had a sappily romantic thought about the cup touching her lips, but pushed it away for a more appropriate thought.

"We need some rain," he said to no one, looking up at the starry sky. He blew air into his cheeks, then sank lower in his chair and blew it out. "Yup, if we don't get some wet soon, the dry's gonna make trouble."

Joleen stopped by the window and looked out. She lingered for a long moment, eyes fixed on something but he couldn't tell what.

Jake lingered too, barely breathing, watching her. "What are you looking for?" Jake asked after a few minutes, but his words were so quiet and light that even the wind didn't pick them up. "Do you *know* what you're looking for?"

She continued to look out; now in the general direction of Jake. He thought at one point he'd caught her eye, but then realized she wouldn't be able to see him in the shadows.

"You're not looking for me, anyway, are you?" He took another gulp of the warm beer and wiped his mouth with the back of his hand. He sighed and tipped his head back, eyes closed. "That's good, Miss Joleen, a lot of folks would call that very good judgment. You stay away from Jake Landon because he's not going where you want to go."

In the distance a dog howled.

He returned his gaze to Joleen. "You want to go to governor's balls and park openings and Washington, D.C. A quiet life in the country, with dogs and kids and early nights and mornings would bore you to death, wouldn't it?" He waited in silence, then heard himself ask, "Would it?"

She turned and picked up a book from her bedside table. She ran her thumb along the spine as she looked at the title. It was a gesture of surprising sensuality.

"You look so alone," Jake said. He was only a little concerned about talking to the wind. Mostly it felt good to be able to say things to Joleen that he'd been wanting to say but couldn't. "Solitude suits you. Carl doesn't belong there with you. If he was there you'd be kowtowing to his every stupid whim, you'd be—" He stopped. He didn't want to think what she might be doing with Carl in the bedroom.

She took a pair of glasses out of a case and put them on.

"You look mighty smart with your glasses on, Joleen. You look smart with them off, too. So why are you making such a stupid mistake with your life?" He noticed the way his own slight Texas drawl lengthened the *I* just a little and it made him laugh. Carl would have corrected Joleen on that mistake. No good Landon could sound like anything other than middle-of-the-road America. His mother had spent years perfecting it herself and trying to cultivate it in her sons.

Carl had always been more of a success story for her than Jake, even in that small way.

"Why would you give up your voice, your words, your conscience and your freedom for a man who can't give you anything more than money?"

The wind rose and brushed past Jake. He saw it lift the curtain in Joleen's bedroom. God, he wanted more than anything to go through that window and take her into his arms. He set the beer down. A little less good judgment and he might do something he'd regret.

He leaned back and crossed his arms in front of him. "That's the one thing I don't understand, Joleen Wheeler. I don't understand why money is so important to a woman like you. You've got everything that really matters in this world and you're giving it all up for...what? If money is all you have, you still don't have anything."

The light snapped off in Joleen's room, and the breeze rose again. Jake inhaled deeply. "I'll tell you one thing," he whispered, leaning back again and closing his eyes. "If you were mine I'd never want you to be anything but yourself."

Joleen was restless. She tried to relax, but she only tossed and turned. Finally she threw the bedcovers back and went to the window seat again, pulling the window as far open as it would go and breathing the fresh air deeply.

It was only a matter of moments before she looked

back over to Jake's place and saw he was still sitting on the porch. She wondered if he'd fallen asleep there when he raised a hand in greeting to her.

Caught! She knew he couldn't read her that well from the distance but she still felt her cheeks burn hot. She waved back, then watched as he slowly stood up and walked across the illuminated stretch of lawn that separated his house from her window. Joleen's heart pounded with every step as he closed the distance between them.

When he got to her window he raised the remains of a six-pack of beer that he had in his left hand. "Want one?" he asked. "They're warm."

"I would." She touched the screen and shrugged.

In one swift movement Jake wrenched the screen off the window frame. "Some problems are easy to solve," he said, handing her a warm can of beer.

She took the beer and popped it open. The foam exploded out and dribbled across her wrist. "Thanks." She shook her arm dry. "You did that on purpose, didn't you?"

He laughed. "I swear on my honor, Miss Joleen, it wasn't a plan. I did the same thing to myself."

"Hmm. Thanks for the warning." She took a sip of the bland, warm foam. She rarely drank, but she did like the earthy, grainy flavor of beer. In fact, it was the secret ingredient of the beef stew at the diner.

Jake dragged a wrought iron chair across the terrace in front of the window and plopped down in it. "So. What are you still doing up?"

"Some strange man came to my window."

"Before that."

"Couldn't sleep." She shifted her weight and rested her elbows on the window frame. "How about you?"

"Same."

She studied him closely but couldn't read the expression in his eyes. Someone else might have called it interest but Joleen knew better than that. The only interest Jake could possibly have in her was as a study in hypocrisy, at least as far as he was concerned.

And that was going to have to stop if she and Carl were going to have any sort of chance at a life together.

"You know, we're going to have to stop arguing," Joleen said, testing the waters.

"We're not arguing."

"I don't mean *now*, I mean in general."

"Ah." He took a long sip. "And why is that?"

She was taken aback. "Because." She thought. How could she put it succinctly? "So there can be some harmony around here, instead of us always being at odds."

"We just don't feel the same way about certain things." He shrugged, calling to her mind the feel of those strong, broad shoulders under her hands. "Why don't we just agree to disagree?"

She shook the idea of his shoulders out of her head. There were more important things on her agenda. "Because we tend to disagree so vehemently."

He raised an eyebrow. She was sure she saw laughter in his eyes. It raised a lump in her throat.

"Then I don't see what we're going to do about that." He met her eyes dead-on. "Unless you're willing to come over to my side and admit I'm right."

She tried to swallow the lump, which had increased with the direct gaze of those blue eyes. "I'm not going to do that."

He gestured broadly with his can. "Now you're just being difficult."

She continued, a little stronger, "Any more than you're going to come over to *my* side and agree that *I'm* right."

He leaned back and appraised her. "So we should *pretend* to agree? For the sake of harmony, as you put it?"

She pursed her lips, then shook her head. "Forget it."

"It's not that I'm not interested in making things as easy and smooth as possible for you and Carl," Jake went on airily.

The mention of Carl's name made her stomach drop. "Of course."

"I'm just trying to help you out."

"Naturally."

He leaned forward and nudged his finger under her chin. His face was just inches from hers, and she could smell the beer on his breath mingling with his masculine scent. "I like you too much to see you make a huge mistake."

She eyed him steadily. "You're about thirty years too late to swoop into my life with that mission now."

He pulled his hand back, giving her chin a light

swipe with his thumb first. Her skin tingled after his touch. "Can't blame a man for trying to do a good deed."

She swallowed. "I guess not."

He stood up, scraping the chair back across the flagstones as he did so. "Time to go." He raised his can to her. "Thanks for the pleasure of your company."

"'Bye," she said softly. As she watched him go she was vaguely aware of an emptiness in the pit of her stomach.

She was lonely.

Joleen rolled over and opened her eyes. The sun glared harshly against the alarm clock.

Alarm clock?

Groggy, she sat up and looked around her. Where was she? She'd been dreaming about a beach, with hot sand and warm water. It took a full minute to remember that she was in the guest room at the Landons' house. She lay back down, pulling the sheets around her. She wanted to return to a lovely dream she'd been having about...what had it been? The details were fuzzy but she knew it had been romantic.

She tried to recall Carl to the scene but every impulse in her rejected the very idea.

Then she remembered.

It had been Jake in her dream. Jake holding her, and kissing her, and telling her that he loved her. Moreover, it had been Jake that Joleen had been holding and loving. She languished in the memory for just a moment, then threw the covers back.

What kind of Freudian dream was that? Obviously Jake had been symbolic of something. She tried valiantly to figure out what he could have been symbolic of, apart from himself. No answer came to her. But that didn't mean anything. Obviously she wasn't *really* having sex dreams about Jake, because that would be, well, just plain wrong.

She got out of bed and stalked to the bathroom and looked at her flushed face in the mirror. Good heavens, she *had been* dreaming about Jake. She'd been dreaming about sex with Jake. He was him and she was her and no one was symbolic of anyone else.

There. The truth may be ugly but it felt better than a lie.

But of all the ridiculous dreams to have! How on earth was she ever going to face Jake again? She turned on the shower and sat down on the toilet, waiting for the water to get hot. The heck with hot, she decided, she needed it cold. Icy cold. She turned the control to the right and stepped into the frigid water with a gasp.

One minute later she stepped back out and wrapped herself in a towel. It was hard to say whether or not the cold water treatment would have any lasting power, but it sure made her stop thinking about Jake for the moment.

She scurried to the bed and jumped back under the sheets, teeth rattling as she shivered. But she warmed up quickly and the smooth sheets and the soft pillow under her head brought the dream back to her with the added notion that Jake was just several yards away, and the feel of his warm body on top of hers would be heaven right now.

"I'm still dreaming," Joleen said to herself. "I would never have such pointless thoughts if I were awake."

Were they pointless? a little voice inside of her asked. Or were they important? She got back out of the bed. Maybe they *were* important. Yes, she'd admit it, she did find Jake attractive. There probably wasn't a woman in America who wouldn't, so that itself didn't make her a bad person. It was acting on it that was wrong. When they'd kissed—a thrill rose in her that he'd been attracted enough to her to kiss her—she'd responded as heatedly as he had.

Was it possible that Joleen was attracted to Jake and *not* to Carl? More importantly, was she willing to give Carl up for Jake?

"Ha! Like someone's given you that choice," she said to herself, then immediately felt a pang of guilt for the betrayal to Carl. She'd never told him she loved him, but she had promised she would come to the ranch to give their relationship a fair shake and see what her feelings were for him.

In other words she'd promised to come to Dallas and try to fall in love with him. He knew it as well as she did.

But he wasn't here. And Jake was.

She went to her suitcase and took out a bra and panties. As she slipped into the bra, she found herself thinking of Jake and she forced her concentration back to Carl.

There wasn't much chance of falling in love with

Carl if she was lusting after Jake. So she'd have to avoid Jake. It was that simple. He'd be leaving in a couple of weeks, anyway. After that it would be a cinch.

After that she'd finally be able to give Carl the chance he'd asked for.

"Besides," she said to herself, slipping on her underwear. "Jake would never be interested in me." She took out her jeans and wrestled them up. "He thinks I'm a sellout or a gold digger. How could he ever have real feelings for me with that idea?"

She went to the closet and took out a white cotton blouse. "He couldn't," she said, in answer to her own question. "If I indulge some silly schoolgirl crush on Jake, I'll risk losing the best thing that ever happened to me. Carl has offered me the only chance I've ever had to get out of Alvira and make something of myself. I'd be a fool to give it up."

She tried to concentrate on buttoning her shirt. She'd go downtown and buy a dress for the Governor's Ball today; that would be a great diversion. She'd pick out the prettiest thing she could find. She'd make Carl really proud of her. Then they'd fall in love and get married and live happily ever after.

And she wouldn't give one more thought to Jake. Not one.

Chapter Seven

Joleen would have done almost anything to avoid another encounter with Virginia Landon, but without a car or a way to get off the property, her only option seemed to be to stay in her suite. And that, she'd already decided, was too close to Jake for comfort.

As she left her room, she saw a note taped to the door. It was from Virginia, marked 8:20 a.m., letting Joleen know that breakfast was served at 8:00 a.m. Joleen looked at her watch. It was nearly nine o'clock. Good. Too late to even wrestle with the question of whether or not she could get out of joining Virginia over crumpets and tea. There was nothing to feel guilty about.

Carl had said there was a car in the garage that Joleen could use for her personal errands, so she set out to find it. The problems began when she couldn't find the garage. After walking the grounds for twenty minutes she realized that what she thought was an entire wing of the house was, in fact, the garage. One peek in the window told Joleen that she was going to have to ask for Jake's help again.

First she tried the guest house, but he didn't answer the door. As she left she noticed a beer can by the chair on the porch. She realized, with a pleasant shiver, that it must be from the previous night when she'd seen him out there.

As she walked back toward the main house, she heard a voice on the terrace and went to look. Virginia and Jake were there, not talking to one another over the remains of toast, orange juice and coffee. Jake was oblivious behind a wall of newspaper, and Virginia was talking on a delicate white telephone.

"Excuse me, Jake," Joleen whispered as she approached.

He dropped the newspaper and looked at her with the very gaze he'd had in her dream. Joleen's heart skipped a beat and her face grew hot. He knew! He knew exactly what she'd dreamed! The corner of his mouth was drawn into the slightest hint of a smile. Was he laughing at her? Were her thoughts not only transparent but also amusing?

No, this was insanity, of course he couldn't read her mind. Still, she had to swallow before she could find her voice again. "I need to go into town, and I was wondering which car I should use." He regarded her, uncomprehending, and she added quickly, "Carl said there was one in the garage, but I looked and there are about fifteen in the garage."

He raised an eyebrow. "You want a ride?" Was she nuts or was there seduction in his voice? His gaze lingered on hers for a moment, then flicked down to the newspaper in front of him. She was nuts. The only place there was seduction was in her mind.

Her heart lurched. "No," she said quickly. "I mean, no thanks. I think I'd enjoy the drive today."

Jake smiled and took a bite of toast. "What do you feel like driving?"

"I'll take whatever car you want me to take," she said. "It makes no difference to me."

"Okay." He set the paper down and popped the last piece of toast in his mouth. "C'mon," he said, chewing.

She followed him across the yard toward the garage she had discovered earlier.

"You sure you want to drive yourself?" Something about his tone told her that he really didn't think she should go out alone.

"Yes, I'm sure." An uncomfortable thought came to her. Maybe he wasn't being protective of her, but was being protective of the car instead. "Unless you're concerned about my driving one of the family's cars."

He kept his eyes focused straight ahead. "I didn't say that."

"You didn't need to." She felt herself bristle and didn't understand it herself. "Don't worry, I'll be very careful."

"I'm not worried." He shrugged. "Blow the damn thing up, for all I care. I just thought you might be more comfortable if I gave you a ride." They stopped at the wall, and he pushed a button that opened the side door. A line of various German cars faced out at her. Jake turned to face her, too, and she was struck by how natural he looked amidst all this elegance. "I don't know why you've got such a chip on your shoulder."

"Maybe it's because from the moment you met me you've been telling me I'm not suited for this life. For Carl."

He didn't even blink. "You're not."

Her blood pressure rose. "How do you know? You don't even know me. And it seems as if you barely even know your brother!"

"Ah, but to know him a little is to know him well." He turned away from her and ran his finger along the rack of keys by the door.

"You know, it sounds to me like you might be jealous of him," Joleen ventured.

That got him. Jake spun to face her with a heated expression. Even his skin was slightly flushed. "What the hell is *that* supposed to mean?"

"Just what I said. The only reason I can think of for you to be constantly putting down Carl is because you're jealous of him."

He'd regained his composure enough to belittle her theory with a humorless laugh. "Sorry, darlin', there's not a thing in this world that Carl is or has that I want for myself." He met her eyes with what looked like defiance. "Nothing."

"Then why do you bother hanging around here, telling me what a jerk he is and how wrong I am for him?"

"Because I feel sorry for you."

"You feel *sorry* for me?" The word stuck in her

throat like a big wad of gum. "I do *not* need your pity, Jake Landon."

"*Pity* is a bit strong, I just meant—"

"That I'm so pathetic that I don't know what's bad for me."

He scoffed. "Hey, I was just trying to do you a favor. Trust me, I've seen the error of my ways. In fact, now that I think about it, with you trying to fit yourself into some mold of what you think he wants you to be, and with him trying to look like the perfect candidate to the voters, you two seem like a match made in heaven."

Joleen felt her own face grow hot. "Carl isn't trying to be anything except a good leader for this state."

"Well then, you don't even know him a little." He turned back to the key rack and snatched a set from one of the brass hooks.

"I know him well enough to marry him," Joleen heard herself say. A sick feeling lodged in her stomach but she continued, anyway. "And spend the rest of my life with him."

Jake looked shocked. "You've made your decision then?"

"Yes. I have." And she sounded like she meant it, too. She surprised even herself with her fervor.

"And that's your plan? To marry Carl and spend the rest of your life with him?"

She couldn't stop. "The sooner the better."

Jake's eyes flicked downward for a moment, and Joleen felt like he took her hopes down with them. Then he looked back up and tossed her the keys. His eyes were devoid of all expression. "Second to the end, Mercedes 450SL. I hope you'll be really happy together."

"The car and I?"

He opened his mouth as if to explain, then just said, "Yes." He walked away and did not look back.

Joleen walked down the line of cars, feeling her insides tremble like gelatin. What had she just done? What on earth had she just *said?* The words, *I know him well enough to marry him and spend the rest of my life with him,* resonated with a dull finality. Spoken aloud, the idea struck actual fear in her heart. It was too soon, too permanent, too…something.

Too drastic. In fact, she wasn't even sure why she'd said it. She'd started that whole argument with him deliberately but she didn't know why. Was she hoping he'd talk her out of staying with Carl?

Or was she hoping he'd talk her into something else?

She got to the car, opened the door and slid in. After a moment of gripping the wheel and trying to return her pulse and breathing to normal, she realized that she wanted Jake's approval. Without it, the idea of marrying Carl didn't seem valid. Every time Jake told her she was wrong for his family it hurt her.

When she was in elementary school, Joleen had been bullied by the popular girls. Finally one day her mother had asked her why she cared what they thought, because she didn't have any respect for them and didn't want to be friends with them anyway. After that, their taunts had meant nothing to her, and soon after that, the taunts had ended.

So why couldn't she do the same thing now? Why couldn't she just decide she didn't give a damn what he thought and ignore him? The difference was that she *did* have respect for Jake. She *did* care what he thought—for some reason she cared a lot.

And even without all that, there was something compelling about him that made her stop and listen to what he had to say. For example, about the corporate bulldozing of mom-and-pop businesses. And about not selling your soul for money even if it does make things easier, not that she was doing that.

Jake Landon was impossible to ignore.

She started the car and pulled out into the driveway. The engine purred like a large, restrained lion. She inhaled the scent of leather and oil soap. *This* was living, she told herself. Maybe some people had to "sell their souls" to enjoy this, but not Joleen. This was the sort of life she'd always dreamed of, and she wasn't going to have to compromise her values to enjoy it.

Any minute now it was going to be tremendously satisfying.

Joleen spent half the day in town, going to all the stores Carl had listed as having "appropriate" clothing. She couldn't find anything she liked, and she definitely couldn't find anything she could afford. Despite the fact that Carl had told her to put it all on account, Joleen didn't feel right about letting him buy her clothes. To her, that felt like one of the last stops before becoming completely dependent. She never wanted to become dependent on someone else.

Finally she went to a chain clothing store in a strip

mall and found a terrific knock-off of Coco Chanel's "little black dress." It was elegant, understated and yet sophisticated enough for Audrey Hepburn. Best of all it was on sale for seventy-nine dollars, which was more than Joleen usually spent on clothes, but far less than she would have spent in one of the other stores she'd been to that morning. She bought the dress and took it out to the car.

So what if it wasn't a thousands-of-dollars designer original? She would wear it well and make Carl proud of her, anyway. There was no "selling out" in that plan. She would be witty at the right times and silent at the right times. She wouldn't miss a step, either on the dance floor or in conversation. She would show Jake Landon she could be just as classy as anyone else there. It wasn't a matter of pretending to be something she wasn't, it was simply a matter of self-improvement.

Of course, she'd show Carl, too. That was her main purpose in being the best she could possibly be. She'd show him his faith in her was justified.

I don't want you to say anything. You just need to smile and look pretty. Carl's words came back to her with horrible resonance. He hadn't wanted her to speak at the park opening because he hadn't wanted her to embarrass him. He didn't have any more faith in her than Jake or Virginia.

She saw a fast-food restaurant in the block ahead and fought the temptation to stop in for a greasy burger with the works. And fries. French fries seemed like just the thing to calm her frazzled nerves. Or maybe a nice, big bowl of chili, with loads of cheese and sour cream.

Might as well do it now. You know when Carl gets back you'll never be able to stop somewhere like that for a bite to eat.

Joleen's hands tightened on the wheel. She couldn't stop. It wasn't because of Carl, or because she needed to lose weight. It was another facet of her new self-improvement. She couldn't pig out on fattening foods every time she hit a little bump in the road. She had to face it and go on.

So she would. Bump number one: Carl's request that she keep quiet. The sheer lack of confidence in her that went into that request was insulting. Of course, he had been right. That was bump number two: as soon as she'd opened her mouth she'd gotten him into a whole heap of trouble. Which made his apparent fear of her making a fool of herself an even bigger wound.

She passed the exit she'd normally take to the ranch and continued driving through town. She wasn't quite ready to face bump number three again: Jake. Especially not with this new realization about Carl undoubtedly written all over her face. She drove on, determined to take a few extra minutes to drive away her worries and tensions.

By the time she got back to the ranch it was early evening. She crept through the house like a thief, trying desperately to avoid running into anyone or having any sort of conversation. She just wasn't up for it. Fortunately, she tried to reason, Carl would be back in a couple of days. They'd go to the Governor's Ball and have a wonderful time and prove to everyone—including Joleen, with any luck—that they were perfect for each other.

When she got to the door to her suite, she saw a note taped to it again.

"What is it this time?" she murmured to herself. "A note telling me I've missed the usual dinner time?" She immediately felt guilty for her sarcasm. No matter how Virginia Landon treated her, that was no excuse to be rude and ungrateful. Her mother would have told her the same thing.

She took the note and pushed the door open, dropping the shopping bag on the windowsill. She turned on the light and looked at the paper in her hand. It was a quick scrawl in a decidedly masculine hand.

Joleen—
    Carl called, left a message that he won't be back until early next week.

                                    Jake

That was it. No explanation, no number to return the call. Just a brief word to let her know she'd be on her own for yet another high-pressure "appearance." She waited for the expected disappointment but it didn't come. Carl wasn't on his way back yet and she was…glad? Good Lord, that was it—she was actually *relieved*.

Joleen sat down. This was bad. This was very bad. She was supposed to be looking forward to seeing Carl. She was supposed to be falling in love with him. She was *supposed* to be rationalizing a way to marry him.

She gasped at the thought. Rationalizing? Yes, that's exactly what she'd been doing. Her hopes began to crumble, her vision of the future faded like a chalk sidewalk drawing in the rain.

"Don't think about this now," she told herself. But she *had* to think about it. She'd been trying to talk herself into something that didn't feel right, and she couldn't turn away and pretend it wasn't true any more.

Tears stung her eyes. She should leave right away, she knew, but she couldn't. She'd be expected to attend the ball in Carl's place. She couldn't just dump him without telling him, and let him find out by learning she'd ditched her responsibilities as well.

Meanwhile there was no way for her to get in touch with him. Well, maybe she could ask Jake or Virginia, but it was a little humiliating to admit to them that Carl hadn't left her with any way to get in touch with him. However, on the chance that that had been a mere oversight on Carl's part, she had to give him the respect of waiting and telling him, first and in person, that she wasn't going to marry him.

She wasn't going to marry him! She let out a breath that made her realize she'd barely breathed for weeks. It was amazingly liberating for all the sadness it caused. She wasn't going to marry Carl.

She couldn't wait to tell him!

But until she did, she couldn't tell anyone. She couldn't humiliate poor Carl that way.

She still had the piece of paper in her hand. She

looked at it, the blessed piece of paper that had somehow stopped her from making the biggest mistake of her life. But it wasn't the paper that had stopped her, it was the note on it, from Jake. *Jake* had stopped her from making that mistake. Okay, it had been Carl's action, but Jake was the messenger.

She studied the writing, looking for the message between the lines. Running her finger across the words, she imagined a lot of things between the lines but saw none of them. It was silly of her to look. Jake had been quite clear about what he thought of her. He'd also made it clear what he thought of his brother, and there wasn't a reason Joleen could think of that he wouldn't suspect her of having the same personality traits he hated in Carl. Or, if not the same, at least complementary ones.

This was silly, trying to decipher what Jake thought of her. It didn't matter. It didn't change things one bit. This was about Carl and Joleen, not about Jake and Joleen.

She crumpled the paper and threw it in the trash can.

He shouldn't have told her that way. She'd be upset when she found out Carl wasn't coming back yet; he should have told her in person. Then he could have at least alluded to some made-up details about what detained Carl and how sorry he was to not make it. Maybe just an extra note: "Have fun!" Like Carl would say.

As it was, Carl had relayed the message to Jake in exactly the clipped, impersonal way that Jake had relayed it to Joleen. Actually Carl had been even less personal than that. Jake didn't think Carl had even used Joleen's name. *Her,* he'd said. *Tell her I won't be back on time.*

Jake shook his head. Why was he trying so hard to protect *her* from Carl? She *wanted* him. She was planning to marry him, to spend the rest of her life with him. She'd told Jake that, in no uncertain terms, herself. Until that moment, he'd been holding out some small hope that it was all a misunderstanding of some sort and she wasn't really planning to marry Carl at all.

Why did he care? After the way she'd dug into him about being jealous of Carl.... *Jealous!* Imagine it!

Okay, well, he could imagine it. Maybe he was just a little bit jealous, but not for the reasons she thought. She thought he was jealous of Carl's inheritance, power, position, or something like that. He'd given all that up long ago. What made him jealous was far more damning.

He was jealous that Carl had met someone as kind and smart and beautiful as Joleen and that she was actually willing to marry him. Jake had never considered himself the marrying kind, but it wasn't hard to imagine sharing the day-to-day details of life with Joleen. Yes sir, a woman like that could make those rough days quite a bit more bearable.

But that wasn't like being jealous of something Carl had accomplished. It was being jealous of something Carl had lucked into. That was different. In fact, that hardly even qualified as jealousy.

He knocked on the door, and Joleen opened it.

"Did you get my note?" Jake asked, knowing full well she had since it wasn't on the door anymore.

Joleen must have thought the same thing because she looked very deliberately at the door where it had been, then back at Jake. "Yes."

He shoved his hands into his front pockets and shifted his weight. "Good. Just wanted to make sure because, you know, the governor's thing is tomorrow night, and I didn't want you waiting around for Carl if he wasn't going to show."

She leaned against the door frame. "You're dying to say it, aren't you?"

"Say what?"

"I told you so."

He raised his eyebrows. "Why would I say that?"

"You know darn well what I'm talking about. This probably confirms, for you, all the wretched things you've been saying about Carl."

"Does it do that for you?"

"He's been detained, that's all. Things like that happen all the time. It doesn't mean he's a bad person."

He laughed. "Not by itself, no. But add it to the list of things he's done this year alone, and you've got a pretty convincing argument."

She didn't smile. "Was there anything else you wanted?"

His eyes flicked briefly into the room behind her. "No. Just wanted to make sure you got the note."

She nodded. "Well, I did."

"Okay, then."

"Thanks." She started to close the door.

He put a hand up to stop it. "Joleen."

She pulled it back and met his eyes. "Yes?"

How that word echoed with unspoken desires. "Never mind," Jake said, turning to go. "Forget it."

He heard her small intake of breath, then a long moment of silence before, "Jake."

He stopped, turned. The rush of adrenaline that coursed through him made his heart pound hard enough to be heard. She could probably hear it now. "Yeah?"

"I...I—" She faltered.

He knew the desire that was in his eyes but he couldn't erase it. "You...?"

"I wanted to say..." She swallowed and shrugged.

"I'm listening." His words could barely be heard over the crush of silence around them.

"Just..." She ran her tongue across her lips in an unconscious gesture that made his groin tighten like a slip knot. "That maybe you were right."

"You're going to have to give me a little bit more to go on here. Maybe I was right about what?"

"About me. Maybe I am too different."

"Too *different?*"

She nodded. "Maybe I can't fit in with you and your family." Her voice was plainly candid, without inflection or emotion.

"I didn't say that—"

She put up her hand to stop him. "You did, and you were right. I'm not classy, like all the women that are going to be at that ball tomorrow night, I'm no charity fund-raiser or Tuesday bridge lady. I can't even *speak* like them, much less act like them.''

This was it. This was his chance to persuade her to leave Carl. He'd been wishing she'd come to this ever since he met her, but now that she had, he couldn't bear to see the hurt in her eyes. He couldn't bear to let her think the wrongness of her relationship with Carl was because of some deficiency of hers, even if it did make her leave him.

"That's not true, Joleen," Jake said. "You're smart and thoughtful and beautiful." He hesitated as she blushed and looked down.

"That's nice of you to say, but even if that's true, it's not enough. I think this is the sort of thing you have to be born into."

"That's absolutely untrue. My parents weren't born into it."

She looked surprised. "They weren't?"

"No. My father built his fortune long after he met my mother. But that's not the issue here, the issue is refinement. Anyone can achieve that, if they want to. What you have is much more important."

"In other words, I don't have *refinement*." She laughed and pushed her hair back from her eyes. "That's just what I'm talking about."

He wanted to touch her hair like she just had. "You have things that are so much more important than that."

"That's right, I can handle dinner orders for eight tables of four at once."

"Seriously, Joleen. You care about people. That makes you the perfect wife for a guy like Carl." He couldn't believe he was actually saying this, but it was true, now that he heard the words. "If Carl's going to make it into office, he could really use a woman like you to remind him of what's important out there. Maybe someone like you could stop him from selling park projects out from under the people who need them."

She stared at him mutely.

But he'd gotten himself going and now he was on a roll. He hadn't even thought of these things himself until he heard himself say them out loud. Maybe they were more important than his simple belief that a person shouldn't try and switch stations in life.

"You're probably perfect for Carl," he concluded, with a dull ache in his chest. "And we're definitely lucky to have you join the family."

"I don't think your mother shares that view," Joleen pointed out. "And I have to ask myself, do I want to spend the rest of my life trying to overcome my *family's* prejudices against me?"

"I'll be proud to say you're my sister-in-law." He tried to smile but the idea of her marrying Carl still drilled a hole in his gut. He'd have to try and remember to look at the big picture.

He thought he heard her catch her breath. "I'd rather you think of me as your friend."

"Of course." He was floundering now. They both knew it. "So stop this talk about not being good enough or classy enough, okay? You're probably going to end up being the one person who could pull the Landon family back together again."

Joleen's face had grown pale. "You don't mean that. Say you don't mean that."

"I do mean it. Carl and I haven't seen eye to eye on one damn thing in years." He didn't add that it had been all Carl's fault. "But with your influence we might just find some middle ground."

Her lower lip began to tremble, and she bit down on it. Something leaped in Jake's chest. He took it as a signal that he'd better get the hell out of there.

"I've gotta go," he said. "But I guess I'll see you tomorrow night."

"Tomorrow night?" she repeated faintly.

"The ball."

"Oh, yes. The ball." She gave a flicker of a smile that looked more distracted than happy. She started to close the door and said, "Then I'll see you tomorrow night at the ball." She shut the door.

But from behind it, Jake could have sworn he heard her add, "Where is a fairy godmother when you need one?"

Chapter Eight

Joleen must have left at the crack of dawn the next morning, because when Jake got up at eight she and the Mercedes were gone. Throughout the day he found himself stopping and wondering where she was.

Not that he cared, he told himself. It was mostly idle curiosity.

As evening drew near he grew concerned that she might not be on time for the governor's event, then wondered why the hell he was concerned about that. What did he care if she went or not?

He didn't. He didn't care at all. What he was feeling was *intense* detachment.

As it turned out, she did make it back on time. He saw her drive in around six p.m. At six-thirty his mother rang his room to tell him she wouldn't be going after all, and that he and Joleen should go along without her. It felt like a rope looped around his throat.

When she came out to meet him the rope tightened. She looked sensational in a simple black dress that showed just enough leg to drive a man insane, and just enough shoulder to show him the way. She wore her hair up in some sort of knot and had simple diamond studs in her ears. That was it for jewelry. Jake couldn't help the swell of pride in his chest. Even without the glittering jewels—or maybe *especially* without them—Joleen was going to outshine every woman at the ball.

They exchanged small, meaningless pleasantries and got into the car together. Her perfume filled the cab in a subtle but persistent way that niggled at his resistance all the way to the governor's mansion.

But they didn't say a word to each other.

Jake noticed that all eyes were on Joleen as they walked into the mansion. One of the first people to approach them, once they were in, was an important state senator, whom Carl had long been trying to persuade to his point of view on several key issues.

The man extended his hand stiffly. "Jake, old boy, how the hell are you?"

"Good, thanks." Jake shook his hand, then swept his arm in the direction of Joleen. "I don't know if you've met Joleen Wheeler."

"Ah, yes, Carl's fiancée."

"We—no, we're not actually *engaged*, we're thinking about it—"

"I've heard so much about you," the man interrupted.

She turned to Jake, who said, "Joleen, this is Senator James McPartland."

She took the hand that was offered her. "Pleased to meet you, Senator."

"Call me Jim," the man instructed. "All my friends do."

She glanced self-consciously at Jake, who gave an almost imperceptible nod. "Okay, Jim."

"So, Joleen," Jim intoned broadly. "I understand you caused a stir at a charity event recently."

Oh, no. "I did?"

"You certainly did."

Her face grew hot. Had news traveled this far, this fast? It was humiliating. "Look, I only did what I thought was right." Her heart was pounding a warning for her to stop, but she couldn't take any more criticism. She felt Jake's hand on her arm but she couldn't be swayed. "Maybe I shouldn't have spoken so soon, but I spent the day in the town hall today and found out that the land has indeed been sold and will be taken over by the new owners after the first of the year." The pressure from Jake's hand increased.

"Joleen," he said in a whisper. "I don't think he means that."

The senator's face was a mask of incredulity. "My goodness, what land? What sale?"

"The land that the park is built on," Joleen said, suddenly uncertain. "Isn't that what you were talking about when you said I'd created a stir?"

"My dear, I simply meant that stories of your

charm and beauty had already made it back to my office.''

"Oh,'' Joleen said faintly. Jake took his hand off her arm and she felt like she might just keel over. In fact, she felt like she *should* just keel over, and end this nightmare of continually saying the wrong thing, to the wrong person, at the wrong time. "Thank you.''

Next to her, she thought she heard Jake muffle a laugh. It was hard to believe he could actually think this was funny, but the coughing fit he had was certainly suspicious.

Jim McPartland frowned and cocked his head. ''I'm interested in what you were saying, though, Joleen. The One Mile Garden project is in some sort of danger?''

She took a deep, steadying breath. "Look, Mr. McPartland, I don't know much about that. All I know is that it seems risky to have a public service like that based on private property. When I was at the hall of records today I came across the deed to a piece of land off Singer Drive.''

"Singer Drive,'' he repeated, scratching his chin like a cartoon of Santa Claus. "I can't think of any large empty lots there.''

"It's a tiny piece of property but workable. When the owner died six years ago he left it to the state, even though the state didn't want it.'' She shrugged, studiously avoiding Jake's gaze, which she could feel burning on her cheek. "It seems like the perfect solution for everyone.''

"By golly, it does. Do you know the details about this land deed?"

"I wrote them down. I could get them to you tomorrow."

"Do that." He reached into his pocket and took out his wallet. "Let me give you my card." He pulled one out and handed it to her. "That's my private line, it comes directly into my office. I'll be expecting your call."

Joleen was flushed with relief. "That's wonderful Mr.—Jim. I'll call you first thing in the morning." She allowed herself one quick look at Jake.

He was open-mouthed, but smiling. His blue eyes were vibrant against the contrast of his dark suit and hair. After a moment he turned his attention to the senator. "Good to see you, Jim, as always."

"Terrific to see you too, Jake. Send my regards to your brother, eh?" He winked.

"I'll do that."

Joleen was about to breathe a sigh of relief when the senator turned to her and asked, "My dear, would you like to dance?"

"Uh, y-yes. Thank you," she said, though she would rather have done almost anything else. Her nerves were strung so tight she was afraid she might snap at any moment. Trying to keep up with these fancy old-fashioned dance steps only made things worse.

As the older man guided her onto the dance floor, the music picked up to a fast waltz. Joleen had enough trouble doing the simple box step she'd learned from a video, but at this pace dancing was nearly impossible.

When Jake broke in she would have been glad to see him, but that was one feeling she wasn't going to allow herself to indulge. He took her hand gently in his and rested his other hand at her waist. The band slowed to a romantic ballad.

Jake bent closer to her. "That was amazing," he said quietly in her ear. "The way you handled the charity land situation."

She ignored the shivers that crossed her skin and ran down her spine. "That wasn't amazing, it was justice."

"I was really impressed."

"That's kind of you to say." Somehow dancing with Jake was as easy and natural as walking. She could have done it all night long. But that was another feeling she wouldn't allow herself to indulge.

He tightened his arm around her waist. "Carl will be pleased that you minimized his role in it. It looks like I completely misjudged you."

"Does it?" She tried to draw back slightly but he pulled her closer instead. "You thought I was just a country bumpkin who didn't have the savvy to try and control the damage."

He made a noise of objection. "Where do you come up with this stuff?"

"Please. You've been telling me that since the moment we met." She tossed her head back. "Truth is, I just didn't want to confuse the issues. Blaming Carl would have deflected the energy that should go into finding another location for the park."

He cocked his head. "Well done. But what I meant was I misjudged your willingness to get involved. I guess when you spend enough time around people who never mean what they say, it comes as something of a shock to meet someone who does. I'm constantly learning something from you, Joleen. You inspire me. You remind me of how important it is to do what's right, not just to say what's right."

"Thanks." She met his eyes, but only for a moment. She wasn't used to being on the receiving end of such a compliment, and the fact that it was Jake saying it made her that much weaker. "So," she said, trying to change the subject. "Speaking of what's right and wrong, when's the big vote?"

"In three days. Monday afternoon."

Just three days. Would Carl be back by then? "Then you're leaving?"

"Then I'm history."

"Not coming back? No cozy Thanksgivings and family Christmases?"

He laughed. "I don't think so. Why, are you going to miss me?"

"Desperately." Her tone was light, playful. He would never know she meant it.

"That's what I thought," he replied in a tone she couldn't quite identify. She glanced at him, but his eyes were scanning the room, not her.

Her heart skipped a beat. It was a warning that she was about to say something that was probably better left unsaid. "Just as I'm sure you'll be missing me." Darn it, there was a question in there, and that flicker in his eyes meant he'd heard it. Once it was out she waited, holding her breath, for his response.

He didn't miss a beat. "There's not a lot I'm going to miss about Dallas. Or Texas in general. Not a lot."

What did that mean? "Surely there's something?" she prodded, wishing to heaven she would stop.

He looked at her then, with a mellowness she hadn't expected in his blue eyes. "There's one thing."

With his hand around her waist he probably felt the acceleration of her pulse. "What's that?"

After a long pause, he said, "Barbecue. There's this place on the outskirts of town, Melva's, and they make the best damn barbecue I've ever had."

"Barbecue."

He nodded. "Of course, they only opened recently, so you'd think it couldn't be that big a deal to me, but..." His words drifted off and he looked down into Joleen's face. "But I'll miss it, anyway."

"But there are other barbecue places all over the country."

He looked into her eyes and, after a moment's pause, said, "Not like that one."

She wet her lips, which suddenly felt tight and dry. "I guess once you've found something you like, it's not that easy to just replace it."

"That's just how I feel." He adjusted his hold on her hand, and she realized her palms were sweating. "Now, Melva's, they might not be the fanciest place, or the most expensive, but it makes no difference to me."

"It doesn't?"

"Nah." They turned around on the floor. "I mean, if you want good food, what do you care if the curtains cost a thousand bucks and came from some boutique in Paris?"

"I guess that doesn't matter if it's the sandwich you're after." *Oh brilliant, Joleen, you're a master of double entendre.* "What," she cleared her throat, "what makes Melva's barbecue so different?"

"Ah." He captured her gaze. His hand flattened against the small of her back and nudged her slightly closer. "There's just the right amount of heat."

Joleen swallowed. "You like it hot?"

He nodded and she saw a muscle tense in his jaw for just an instant. Then the tension disappeared and his mouth curled into a half smile. "I like it hotter than most. They seem to understand that there. At Melva's."

Her breath caught in her throat. She knew she should get out of there or at least shut up, but she could do neither. "I agree."

His gaze shifted to her mouth. "I thought you might."

"I'm not sure we're talking about barbecue."

They did another turn and the next thing she knew, he was murmuring into her ear. "Now, Miss Joleen, what else would we be talking about?"

His words tickled down the side of her neck. She drew a long breath in, unsure of whether or not he was serious. If he was, then she'd really just stuck her foot in it. "Nothing else," she said. "Just food."

"Nothing wrong with that." His fingers moved in

a tiny trail across the small of her back, and she barely managed to suppress a gasp.

"Oh, jeez, Jake—"

The music stopped and the people around them gave a loud round of applause for the band. Joleen and Jake merely stared at each other for a long minute, before he asked, "You were saying?"

She bit down on her lip and shook her head. "It was nothing."

She started to turn away. He reached for her but didn't touch. "Are you sure?"

"Yes, it was nothing." She attempted a nonchalant shrug. "I can't even remember."

He couldn't respond before Jim McPartland swooped in on them, with another man, who was tall and extremely thin. "Joleen, I'd like you to meet my good friend, Harold Binchey, of Binchey Construction. Hal, this is Carl Landon's fiancée, Joleen Miller."

"Wheeler," Joleen corrected, then smiled. Miller, Wheeler, one peasant was the same as another to the Dallas elite.

Hal Binchey already had his bony hand wrapped around hers. "Ms. Miller, it is a pleasure to meet you. Tell me, when is the big day?"

She knew, with immediate apprehension, what he was talking about. "Big day?" she hedged.

"Yes, when are you and Carl going to make it official?"

She felt, rather than saw, Jake take a step backward. "I...I...we haven't...I don't know."

"Don't tell me he's got cold feet with such a lovely lady as yourself," Hal said.

"No." Out of the corner of her eye she saw Jake. She wanted to tell him the truth, that she wasn't going to marry Carl, but it would have been terribly insensitive for her to do that to Carl. Where she came from, people acted fairly, even when it wasn't easy. And when one person wasn't going to marry another person, that other person had the right to know it before anyone else did.

The men continued to ask questions about the engagement and give what they undoubtedly believed were flattering comments about Carl's good fortune. Joleen listened as graciously as she could.

When Jake excused himself and walked away, her spirits deflated like a discarded balloon. Would she have the chance to end things with Carl before Jake left town? Would it make a difference to Jake one way or the other? Probably not, but for some reason it was important to her that he know.

The rest of the evening passed in a blur. She was aware of Jake in her peripheral vision all night, but they didn't get close enough to talk again. Meanwhile, one person after another approached her for the details of her engagement.

Finally, around eleven o'clock, Joleen decided that she couldn't possibly take any more. She'd fulfilled her responsibility to come and she'd talked with all the people she was expected to meet. Even Carl couldn't ask more of her than that.

She searched for Jake and finally found him surrounded by skinny debutantes with turned-up noses.

If she hadn't been feeling so out of place already, that sight would surely have done it for her.

"Excuse me," Joleen said, hating the way her scalp prickled when the women turned to scrutinize her. "Jake, I just wanted to let you know I'm going to leave now."

Her self-consciousness was eased considerably as he said, "Let me take you."

"No, thanks, you don't need to give me a ride."

He looked immediately concerned. "How are you going to get back?"

She made a face. "I'm a big girl. I'll take a cab." She turned to go.

He followed and caught her, letting the women drop off him like autumn leaves off a tree. "Joleen, let me drive you."

"No," she said, more sternly. "Ever since I came here you've had to do one thing after another for me. I can take care of myself."

"I don't mind—" he started.

"But I *do*." Several people around them stopped talking and watched. She continued in hushed tones. "I don't like feeling indebted all the time. I don't like feeling dependent." The words, as they came to her, made her feel stronger. Things could never work with Carl and this was exactly why. Simply clarifying her feelings made her know she was doing the right thing. "I'm not the sort of person who can let everyone else take care of things for them and make decisions for them, and pick clothes for them." She looked at him a little breathlessly. "Do you understand that?"

"Completely." She wasn't sure whether the look in his eye was admiration or condescension.

"Good," she said, anyway. "Then I guess I'll see you later. I'm going to go off on my own and be by myself for a while."

"Enjoy yourself."

She watched him, looking for the break in his visage that would tell her what he was thinking, but he continued his even perusal. "I will. Goodbye."

"'Bye," she heard him call behind her.

As soon as she got outside, the cool evening air renewed her. Inside, it had been hot and stuffy and the air had been thick with heavy perfumes. Outside, even the light smell of exhaust seemed like fresh air.

She hailed a cab and asked the driver to take her to the best chili joint in town. "Someplace the locals know about but the tourists don't," she specified.

When he pulled up outside Jingles fifteen minutes later he said, "Yer sure you want to go here? Fergive me, but yer a mite overdressed."

"Then this is *exactly* where I want to be," she sighed. She doubled his tip and he left with a cheerful toot of the horn.

Inside, Jingles was exactly the sort of place she'd been hoping to find. The wood floor was rustic and scuffed, the walls were decorated with things that obviously had significance to the owner and hadn't just come from a salvage yard: there were ribbons from horse shows, most bearing the same name, photos of people who looked like they must all belong to one family, and several yellowed newspaper articles about the food, carefully placed behind cheap glass frames.

Several people looked at her clothing askance, but none of the looks made her as uncomfortable as she'd been at the ball. She was at home and it felt, if not great, at least real. There was a lot to be said for feeling real.

She sat down at the bar and ordered a domestic beer from the tap, then she leaned back and soaked in the ambience. The beer was delicious after the bone-dry champagne she'd been sipping at the ball. She drained her mug and ordered another. What the heck? She reached for the chips, too. Might as well go all the way with her decadence. It felt good to be herself again. When the jukebox started playing "Crazy" she nearly laughed.

Then she thought of Jake and her near laughter turned to near tears. She *was* crazy. Crazy to be thinking of him at all, much less fantasizing about him and replaying his meaningless flirtation in her head over and over again.

She ordered another beer. There was a quarter in the change and she took it and the beer over to the jukebox. Until a few weeks ago "Crazy" had been one of her favorite songs. Now it came too close to the truth for comfort. She looked over the selections for something more innocuous. At least ninety percent of the songs were about unrequited love.

As she stood there, trying to find something that was neither depressing nor the Bee Gees, a squat man in a cowboy hat nudged her aside and dumped some change in the machine. He walked away and Hank

Williams' "Your Cheating Heart" wailed at Joleen from the speakers.

She turned away, visions of Jake so strong now she thought she could see him, in the doorway, greeting the regulars. Maybe she shouldn't have had all that beer on an empty stomach. She almost imagined she could hear his deep voice and the husky sound of his laughter. She even felt the shock of recognition as the imaginary "Jake" looked up and caught her eye....

She squinted. *Was* that an imaginary Jake? Or had God played the ultimate trick on her and sent him here? Of all places, they both ended up at the same hole in the wall. With three other restaurants on this block alone, the odds against it were astronomical. How on earth was she going to be able to face him now?

She downed the last of her beer and slipped behind a couple who were slow dancing on the peanut-shell-strewn dance floor. Sure anyone behind her might have thought she was nuts, swaying with the couple to keep from being seen, but it was what was in *front* of her that she was concerned with. Unfortunately her hiding place wasn't as good as she thought it was.

"Joleen?"

He was there, before her, in all his blue-eyed, unbuttoned tuxedoed glory. And he was looking at her. No, not *at* her, right *into* her, right into her soul. He knew her inside out, he had from the start. The biggest mistake she'd made was trying to hide it from him.

"Hello Jake, how are you?" she said, but it sounded, even to her own ears, like "Hijack, how ya doin'?"

The corner of his lips turned up in that way that drove her crazy. "Have you had a little something to drink?"

"Just a couple of beers."

"A cup labeers?" he queried.

She tried to narrow her eyes at him, but concentrated instead on standing still. "Yes."

He studied her, a slow smile creeping across his features. A slow song started. "How about a dance?"

"I don't think we should—"

"Excellent." He swept her into his arms and out onto the floor.

"Jake," she said, but her voice was muffled against his shoulder. She tilted her face up. "Jake?"

He looked down at her. His lips were just inches from hers. "Yeah?"

"I...I..." Her voice was so quiet he bent even closer.

"What's that?"

"I don't think we should be doing this." But she couldn't stop. His body was warm along the length of hers, and comforting, like a pillow that was hard to leave in the early morning.

"What, dancing? Or enjoying it?"

"Who said I was enjoying it?" The temptation to lay her head against his shoulder and sink into the pleasurable oblivion of their synchronized movements was almost irresistible.

"Do you want to stop?" he asked.

"Yes." She didn't move away.

"Okay." He readjusted his arm around her waist, but didn't let go.

They kept dancing.

"Well, I'm glad we got that over with," Joleen said with a small giggle.

"It's nice to hear you laugh," Jake said softly. "That hasn't happened much since you've been at the house."

"You noticed that?" She looked at him in surprise. It hadn't even occurred to her until she heard the truth ringing in his observation.

"I noticed."

"Sorry." She smiled gently. "Didn't mean to be glum."

"I never use the word *glum*." He smiled and she couldn't help but marvel at how good-looking he was. He was by far the best-looking man in the room.

It was on the tip of her tongue to ask how he managed to go about life with such conspicuous good looks when he spoke again. "You should have heard McPartland going on about you after you left tonight."

"Saying what a meddler I am?"

Jake shook his head. "He said you were a rainmaker, you make things happen instead of just talking about them." He tightened his hand around hers. "I agree with him."

"You wouldn't say that if you knew what a mess my personal life was."

He frowned. "What do you mean?"

"There's just so much to do, and I don't know where to start or how long it's going to take to get there." She hesitated. "For instance, college. I've been plugging away at it for what seems like my whole life, but I'm still years from being finished and actually getting started on something meaningful."

"You don't need to finish school to do something meaningful."

She gave a wry laugh. "I wish that were true. It's easy to take education for granted when you've had the opportunity to go."

"You're *assuming* I went to college."

"Did you?"

"Yes—"

She cocked her head. "There you go."

"I had some college," he went on, calmly. "But I don't use it at all now, so it was basically a big waste of time and money."

"At least you have that choice."

"You have it, too. Take what you did today, for instance. You didn't need a degree for that—you went out, researched the records and found a solution to an important problem. You could be doing that every day, instead of working at a job you hate while you struggle to get through—" He stopped abruptly. "What am I saying? I forgot for a minute there that you're marrying Carl. All of this is a moot point."

She opened her mouth to object, but couldn't. At this point he probably wouldn't even hear her anymore, he'd pegged her so completely. The song ended and they pulled apart in silence.

It seemed, for both, there was nothing left to say.

Chapter Nine

As they drove up the long driveway to the house, Jake noticed that the lights were on in the barn. "That's strange."

"What?"

He glanced at the clock on the dashboard. "It's nearly two o'clock in the morning and the light's on down there."

"Maybe Ray left it on accidentally."

Jake swung the car down toward the barn with a feeling of uneasiness. "Maybe." He pulled up by the door, and they got out of the car.

Jake and Joleen walked into the dimly lit barn. "Anyone here?" Jake called.

"Jake?" Ray returned, poking his head out from Trouble's stall. "Man, am I glad to see you."

Heart pounding, Jake rushed over. "What's going on?"

"Colic," Ray answered, gesturing toward Trouble. "Looks bad. I've been trying to get ahold of you all night."

Jake peered in. The normally lively bay Thoroughbred was hanging her head low and stumbling around in her stall. Her legs trembled as she tried to drop to the ground and roll to relieve her discomfort.

"Has she gone down at all?" Jake asked quickly.

Ray ran a hand across his pinched face. "Been trying pretty damn hard."

Jake nodded. If the animal followed her instinct to throw herself down and roll, it would probably twist her intestine, causing a rupture. Then it would be nearly impossible to save her. "What have you given her so far?"

Ray named a couple of medicines. "But I didn't want to give her any more for fear she'd burst something."

"How about something for the pain?"

"Chloral hydrate. Only a little."

"You did the right thing," Jake murmured, slipping his hand behind the horse's front leg to feel for the pulse. It was weak. "Have you taken her temperature?"

"Nearly 103 about twenty minutes back," Ray answered.

Jake let out a long breath and examined Trouble's eyes. "Her eyes are too red," he said, more to himself than to Joleen and Ray. "I don't like this at all."

Ray shook his head resignedly and clicked his tongue against his teeth.

"Could you hand me the medicine kit from the

tack room?'' Jake asked Joleen, who was standing by, looking alarmed. ''It's on the cabinet.''

''Yes.'' She looked grateful for the opportunity to do something.

Ray watched her go, then said, ''I tried Dr. Scully, but he's out of town. Maybe I should have called the fellow who's covering for him, but I kept thinking I could knock this thing out of her. Now if she doesn't make it, it'll be my own damn fault.''

''Ray, come on.'' Jake looked at him and noticed the puckered bags under the man's eyes. ''This isn't your fault. You did everything you could.''

Joleen handed him a black leather bag. ''This?''

''Yeah, that's it.'' He opened the medicine kit and took out a syringe. ''How long have you been at it?'' he asked Ray.

''I started about six this evening.''

Jake halted, mid-motion. ''Good God, old man, you need some rest.'' He spoke with an energy he didn't feel. ''Why don't you go on in now, let me take over?''

''Nah.'' The older man waved the idea away. ''I'm not worth my salt if I can't stay up in an emergency like this.''

''Both of you should go,'' Jake said, taking the cap off the vial and glancing from Joleen to Ray. ''I'll call you if I need help.''

''I'd rather stay here and help,'' Joleen said. Jake was surprised how soothing he found her words. ''If nothing else I can get coffee and keep talking to keep you awake.'' She turned to Ray. ''But you should go, really. You look exhausted. Besides, I know a thing or two about horses and colic and if you're going to have to walk Trouble all night to keep her from lying down and twisting her stomach, you're going to need to take over the morning shift so you don't both drop.''

Good point, Jake thought. She had a way of making people feel needed and useful. He noticed the light that came into Ray's eyes as he said, "Yes, that's true.''

"You'll have to be alert," she finished.

He nodded. "I can see your point. But you'll call if you need anything?''

"Absolutely," Jake said, aware, despite his worry, that when Ray left, Jake and Joleen would be alone together at the scene of the kiss. He shouldn't have been thinking of that at a time like this but he couldn't help it.

"All right," Ray said with resignation. Jake noticed he looked relieved. "But—''

"No *buts,*" Jake said. "Go.''

When Ray had gone Jake glanced at Joleen, then drew the medicine from the vial into the syringe. "Good work. If you hadn't thought of the morning shift, Ray would have killed himself to stay up and see this through.''

"I don't know how he did it this long, he's out here at five in the morning.''

Jake stopped and raised an eyebrow at her. "And how do you know that?'' Her face colored and he said, "Joleen if you've been up since five you have no business being out here, either.'' He shook his head. "What a bunch of martyrs.''

She laid a hand on his arm. "I want to help, Jake."

"You're not going to be any damn help if you fall asleep on me."

"I won't fall asleep on you," she said. "If you won't fall asleep on me."

What would he give for the opportunity to do just that? "I'm not tired."

"Good. Neither am I."

He adjusted the syringe, then pinched the skin at Trouble's neck, and injected a sedative into it. Joleen was right; he would need some help, at least until he'd finished with what he was doing. "Easy, girl," he said gently to the horse. He emptied the vial, then followed quickly with a saline infusion to prevent the animal from going into shock. The horse nickered weakly.

Jake examined her further. The pulse was still weak. That was the worst sign. "I need to do more," he said, thinking. The answer came to him. "Keep her up while I get some liquid paraffin and a stomach tube out of the back."

He went to the tack room and paused for a moment when he was inside the door. If he lost this mare... It didn't bear thinking about. He couldn't lose her, that was all there was to it. He just couldn't lose her. If this mare died it would feel like an omen over his horse-breeding career. He wasn't sure he'd be able to get over that idea. He grabbed the equipment and went back out to get it ready.

Joleen turned to Jake, as he pumped oil into the stomach pump. "I know how important this is to you. For what it's worth, I'm praying."

He was so touched by her concern that he could barely find his voice. "Couldn't hurt."

"That's a good girl, easy does it," she said, resting her hand on Trouble's withers. "How do you know how to do all this?" she asked Jake.

"Went to school for it."

"What? You mean, you're a vet?"

"I don't practice."

"But you went all the way through veterinary school?"

She sounded so shocked he had to laugh. "Yeah, I did."

"You didn't tell me that. *Some college,* you said, you had *some college.* You didn't mention a medical degree."

"It didn't strengthen my point. I was trying to emphasize to you that it doesn't matter what you study in college if you're already equipped to do something else."

She laughed. "Good Lord, is there anything else? Are you a dentist on the side?"

"No." He clapped the horse on the shoulder and stood up. "I quit in my last year of dental school."

For just a moment she looked like she believed him. Then she smiled. "So how come you don't use your degree?"

Jake finished and removed the long tube. He looked at Joleen. "Not enough money in it."

She frowned. "Money isn't everything, I've heard."

He opened his case again and took out another syringe. "What idiot told you that?"

"A very wise man," she answered, a little wistfully. Their eyes met, and in that small moment he imagined he saw the future in her eyes.

"Don't believe everything you hear. Most people don't know what the hell they're talking about, ever." He injected a muscle relaxant into the horse's neck again. "There." He gave Trouble a pat and turned to Joleen. "You wait with her while I clean the tube, all right?"

"Okay." As he disappeared out of sight, she called, "What's the real reason you don't practice?"

"I did, for a while." There was a clattering sound. "But it didn't work out."

"Didn't work out? What does *that* mean?"

He came back out. "If I tell you, will you promise to stop hammering at me?"

She raised her hand. "I promise."

"I made a mistake. Lost a hundred-thousand-dollar Thoroughbred—someone else's, by the way—because of my stupid mistake." He gave a shake of his head. "I'm not the sort of guy who should be entrusted with lives."

"Anyone can make a mistake."

"Would you go to a doctor for surgery if you knew he'd made a fatal mistake, even once?"

Her silence was all the answer he needed.

"Exactly. Now, let's consider the matter closed."

"But—"

"Ah-ah-ah, you promised. Now, wait here, I have to get something out of the car."

As soon as Jake was gone, she closed her eyes and leaned into Trouble. "Please. You've got to make it,'' she whispered. ''He needs this. You've got to pull through.''

By the time Jake came back, Trouble was looking considerably better. The trembling that had shaken her body had ceased, and her eyes had lost some of the wild, tortured look they'd had when he'd gotten there.

''She looks better, doesn't she?'' Joleen asked exuberantly.

''She does.'' His words were weighted with caution.

''So, is everything all right now?''

''She's not in the clear yet,'' he said. ''She's just drugged. Now I've got to walk her and wait with her. Could be a long time. You really should go on in, now, and get some sleep.''

''So should you.''

''I can't.''

''Then neither can I.'' Her lips curled up at the corners.

''Okay.'' Jake grinned, despite himself. Her smile was beguiling, and the way her eyes shone with relief got him, right in the pit of his stomach. She was more beautiful than ever.

''You said most people don't know what they're talking about most of the time,'' Joleen said. ''Did you mean anyone in particular?''

''Everyone.''

''You?''

''Especially me.''

''But you're the one who told me to be true to myself.''

"You could have gotten the same advice from a fortune cookie. It's not that profound."

She looked down. "I thought it was."

"If you're of a mind to take advice, Joleen, you should get it from someone who knows something about all this man-woman stuff." He gave a wry laugh. "I'm in the dark."

"And glad to be there, from the sound of it," Joleen said.

"You bet," he said, a little too vehemently. "I need a woman in my life like I need a hole in the head."

Joleen gaped at him in stunned silence for a moment, then asked, "So, should I walk her some, while you put all your tubes and needles away?"

"Yeah, that'd be great," he said. "I've given her everything I can for the time being."

She opened the stall door and led Trouble out slowly. Jake paused and listened to the familiar clop-clop on the cement. He glanced at her retreating form and ached at the sight of Joleen, still in her evening gown and shoes, now muddied, leading the horse out into the night. "Watch your step out there in the dark," he called. "We don't need another casualty."

She looked back at him. "Don't worry about me," she returned coolly. "I can take care of myself."

Their eyes met and held in the soft golden light in the barn. All of Jake's resolutions about Joleen dissolved like steam. His head was shouting warnings that his heart didn't hear, and it made him furious. He wasn't the sort of guy who went after another man's woman, especially his brother's. Granted, that wouldn't have stopped Carl from doing the same thing but that's where they were different. And that difference was really important to Jake. He watched Joleen walk into the darkness with the horse, and leaned back against the wall for a moment.

He *had* to stay away from her, he told himself.

"Wait up a second," he called instead. "I'll go with you."

Wordlessly, they walked out into the cool, clear night, Trouble clopping along between them like a metaphor for their insurmountable odds. The barn was on the crest of a gentle hill, and it was there that they walked, back and forth while minutes turned silently to hours. They returned to the barn a few times throughout the night, so that Jake could repeat doses of sedatives and muscle relaxants with the hope of giving the mare some genuine relief.

It was long in coming and so they continued to walk in the cold, clear darkness. Sometime past four-thirty in the morning, Jake said, "You did great tonight. All that stuff about the parkland...I was really impressed."

She shrugged, and kept her eyes straight ahead. "I just did what I promised I'd do."

"You put me to shame."

She jerked her head in his direction. "Put *you* to shame? How so?"

"With all my talk about how wrong that sort of business practice is, I've never in my life done anything to try and right it. It never even occurred to me."

They ambled along in silence for a few more

minutes, then Joleen said, out of the blue, "Are you against all marriage, or just the idea of Carl's?"

Carl's and yours, he amended silently. "I'm not against marriage at all," he said. "It's just not something I'd ever want to do."

"Never?" she asked quietly.

"Never," he answered. "Why buy the cow?"

"That's an ugly sentiment."

He shrugged, even though she couldn't see him in the dark. "It's true. Men and women are good for each other in some ways. Don't get me wrong, I'm just as willing to give as I am to receive."

"But there are limits to how far you'll go on both ends," she interjected.

He hesitated. "In some ways, yes." But there was only one limit he wouldn't push to be with Joleen. That limit—Carl—stood in the way of all other possibilities. Which was for the best, really, since he wasn't the marrying kind. He didn't realize he'd said the last part out loud until she questioned him.

"What, exactly, *is* the marrying kind?"

"I guess that would be a guy who could settle down with one girl and never look at another one." He looked at her and felt a pang in his chest. "Seems to go against nature, but there you have it."

"Marriage goes against nature."

He nodded. "That's right."

"So all the people who have lived on this earth over the past thousands of years were all going against nature."

"Okay, it's against *my* nature. Is that better?"

He could have sworn she said no, but when he

asked her to repeat herself she just said, "It's fine. Whatever."

Another quiet moment passed, and they resumed their walking. "Do you think we're making any progress here?" Joleen asked, patting Trouble's shoulder.

For a moment he thought she was talking about the two of them, then he realized she was referring to the horse. "Time will tell. She's looking more comfortable."

"I think so, too," she agreed. "Looks like you worked a miracle."

"Not me."

"Come on, if it weren't for you, she'd probably be—" She didn't finish the sentence, but the word *dead* hung between them as certainly as if she had. "Looks like your education paid off in a big way."

"We weren't going to talk about that."

"Okay."

"Anyway, Trouble's the one doing all the work now," Jake said. "Keep your faith in her, not in me."

They had been walking for what seemed like ages. The sun was peeking up at the eastern sky when the horse stopped short.

"What's wrong?" Joleen's voice was thin with worry. Dark circles like smudges lined her eyes.

Jake ran a hand through his hair, scanning his weary brain for the words he would say if the animal dropped to the ground. "She's probably as tired of walking around as we are."

He laid a hand on Trouble's shoulder then felt the

pulse. It was stronger now than it had been. Then the muscles tightened and the horse strained. Jake frowned. "Come on, girl," he said, drawing her forward a few steps. He looked at Joleen and tried desperately to think of something to send her into the barn for. He didn't want her to be here if the worst happened. "There's a red horse blanket in the white trunk in there. Can you get it?"

"A *blanket?*"

His tired mind chugged slowly. He didn't have a clever follow-up. "I don't want her to get a chill," he said lamely.

"Okay." Joleen dashed toward the barn, heedless of her fancy dress. He watched her go and felt another pang in his chest.

Jake turned back to the horse, dread and hope at war in his heart. "Okay, girl. What's it going to be?"

The seconds ticked by with what felt like an unreal sluggishness before the answer finally came and the horse passed the impaction.

By the time Joleen got back with the heavy wool blanket, both Jake and Trouble were better.

"What is it?" Joleen asked. "What's happened?"

"Let's just say she's over the worst," Jake said, smiling. He gestured at the ground nearby and Joleen nodded. "I think she's going to be all right now."

Joleen was smiling, too, and rubbed her hand across Trouble's neck. "Oh, that's such good news." Her expression held a lightness that Jake hadn't seen before. "So the drama is over?"

"Probably so," Jake said carefully. "With a little luck and some antibiotics." They led the horse into the barn and Jake gave her yet another injection in the neck.

"She looks so much better," Joleen marveled. "Quite a bit better than we do right now. No offense, but you look like hell."

"You're looking a little tired yourself." Jake reached his hand out and brushed a finger across her cheek.

She smiled into his eyes. "But I feel great."

And she looked great. The temptation to lean over and kiss her was almost overwhelming. But he knew that the kiss would be wrong.

They stood, inches apart, looking at each other. He replayed their earlier conversation in his head and it strengthened his resolve just in the nick of time. One more moment and he would have thrown caution to the wind and kissed her.

"Well," he said, "I'm going to give Ray a little wake up call so he can get his butt out here and relieve us."

Joleen hesitated. "I'll put Trouble in her stall and make sure she's got some water."

"Thanks. Make sure there's no food in there at all," Jake said, watching her lead his future away. "Or hay."

"All right."

Jake made a couple of calls then came back to the stall, with a heavier heart than he'd had all night.

"Good news for you," he called to Joleen, completely without enthusiasm. She was sitting on an overturned water bucket, head in hands.

She raised her head and stifled a yawn. "What?"

"Carl's back."

That woke her up. Her eyes flew open wide. "Where?"

Jake gestured vaguely. "He's up at the house right now, probably wondering where the devil you are."

"Oh." She stood immediately, smoothing her hands across her hopelessly dirty dress. "Is he waiting for me?"

"Don't knock yourself out. He's eating breakfast and making a few calls." *He's not in the hurry to see you that I would be in his place.*

Her shoulders dropped fractionally. Relief? Or despondency? "Oh. Okay."

"Joleen..."

"Yes?"

He pinched the bridge of his nose and tried to clear his thoughts. The feeling between them just wasn't right. His stomach was aching; he felt weak. He had to say something to alleviate this tension between them, but he didn't know what. "I don't want you to misunderstand what I was saying before, about relationships. I mean, I don't want you to think I'm a jerk or anything."

She shrugged and shook her head. "You don't owe me any explanations. And I don't think you're a jerk."

"I just don't look at it with the same romantic vision you have," he said. "I wish I could."

"You don't know how I look at it." Her voice was almost childlike in its simplicity. "How can you make a judgment like that, saying I have this dreamy view of marriage, when you don't even know me?"

"Maybe I know you better than you think," Jake said quietly.

Joleen stared at him and he felt his chest tremble. "Maybe you know me less than you think."

He felt a little like the devil facing a wooden cross. "You're right." He waved the notion off. "What do you care what I think, anyway? You've got more important things to worry about."

Her eyes were unusually bright. "What if I do care?"

"Then you're in trouble." He stepped toward her. "I'm not a people sort of person."

"Just a loner, huh?"

He lowered his chin and studied her. She shifted her weight nervously but continued to look him in the eye. "I suppose you don't need anyone or anything."

"That's right."

She eyed him steadily. "You'll just go off into the sunset after this board meeting and spend the rest of your life in solitude, punctuated by the occasional dalliance here and there and that's going to make you happy."

"That suits me." It suited him like a death sentence. "What about you? You want to tell me about how much better your life is going to be here in Dallas?" he asked, longing to reach out and smooth her hair back, to touch her cheek. "Political rallies, womens' club lunches, silent auctions, standing around looking pretty?"

"You think I can't do it."

"You shouldn't care what I think. What do *you*

think? Is it worth marrying for money when it comes with all that?'' He waited in silence for her reaction.

"I would only marry for love," she said with quiet emphasis.

One more step all but closed the gap between them. "Do you love Carl?"

Again, she looked down and he knew he had his answer. He reached out and cupped his hand under her chin, raising it gently so she looked him in the eye. "You don't love Carl," he said, placing his other hand on her shoulder and gently pulling her toward him.

She kept her gaze on his, moving as though in a hypnotic trance. Jake put both hands on her shoulders, and the feel of her warm flesh under his shot a flaming arrow right through him. He ran his thumbs gently across her skin. Her perfume—something powdery smelling—wafted up with the heat and mingled with the barn smell, singling her out as the sweetest thing there. "Have you ever been in love, Joleen?''

She swallowed, still looking into his eyes. "I...I don't know.''

"Then how do you know that even that is worth marrying for?" He pulled her closer and lowered his lips onto hers. The heat of passion that washed over him was a surprise. The moment their lips touched it was as if an electric shock jolted through him. His fingers tightened on her shoulders, and he realized vaguely that he was willing her to stay, not to pull back.

She lifted her arms to rest on his shoulders and

tangled her fingers in his hair. The gesture was sooth-ing, encouraging. This was *right*.

Her mouth parted under his and he deepened the kiss, aroused by the sounds and the taste of the kiss. He ran his hands slowly down her sides, then circled them around her waist, drawing her closer still, press-ing her against him.

She ran her hands down his shoulders and sides, slowly, as if every inch mattered. It did. He came alive under her touch. These were sensations he hadn't felt in years—or had he ever? He couldn't remember. All he knew was that the moment he'd first laid eyes on her, he'd felt something drawing him to her. Now he knew it was mutual.

Joleen trailed her hands across his stomach then flattened her palms against his chest, meeting his pas-sion with tender kisses and a tentative flick of her tongue against his.

Jake's hands eased down to the small of her back. She was exquisite. Her soft body molded perfectly against his and was deliciously warm against him, even on the hot summer morning.

Suddenly he felt her fingers clench against him, and she pushed off. "What are you *doing?*" she cried, her face flushing to a deep red.

"I'm doing the same thing you are."

She raised her hands to her cheeks. "We can't do that."

"Why not?" Jake asked stupidly. He felt like he was freefalling from an airplane, and collecting his wits was not an easy thing.

"Carl," she sputtered. "I can't—we can't—my God, what if he came in and saw that? It's *wrong*."

"It didn't feel wrong to me," Jake said, knowing as well as she did that it *was* wrong.

She shook her head. "That shouldn't have happened." Her voice wavered. "Not now."

He took a long breath. "Then when?"

"Never." She looked at him fiercely. "I'm not the dalliance kind."

For a moment he didn't know what she was talking about. Then the light came on. "That's right, you're the marrying kind, aren't you?"

She clicked her tongue against her teeth. "How do you do that?"

"Do what?"

"Make it sound so pathetic. The *marrying kind,* like it's something to be ashamed of."

How could he tell her the shame was his and not hers? That he'd entertained the idea of turning his back on his family for her and it hadn't felt so bad. That he'd come within inches of putting her in the awkward position of the middle of a family feud because he couldn't control his own damn feelings. "We've talked about that already."

She looked at him for one hard minute then shook her head disgustedly. "Don't worry, I won't drag you back through it. If you'll excuse me, I'm going to see Carl."

"By all means, go to Prince Charming."

She reeled around hotly. "I need to talk to him."

Jake raised his hands in surrender. "I understand."

"No, I don't think you do, I have to—" She broke

off and he saw she was kneading her hands in front of her.

"You okay?" he asked, suddenly concerned. He hadn't seen her this distressed before.

She followed his gaze to her hands, then dropped them at her side. "I will be, as soon as I'm out of here."

This had really upset her, and for that he was sorry. "Look, we'll forget what just happened. We're tired and punchy. We probably lost a lot of judgment along with all the sleep."

She nodded but didn't look convinced. "I'm going to go see Carl now."

Jake took a few steps after her. "Joleen, wait."

She stopped and turned back. "What?" Her voice was pleading, almost desperate.

He floundered, looking for something—anything—to say. Words failed him. "Never mind."

With one final, lingering gaze, she nodded and turned away.

With an empty heart, he watched her walk back to the house, and to Carl.

Chapter Ten

Joleen's feet felt like they were made of lead. Every step took her closer to the house and closer to freedom...and further away from Jake. On top of that, she had no job, no place to live, and forty-two dollars to her name. She pressed on, telling herself that as difficult as this was going to be, it was ultimately for the best.

Except the part about being further away from Jake. That part made her feel strangely lonely.

She went in the kitchen door, expecting to encounter Carl right away. When he wasn't there she panicked. Her rhythm had been thrown off. Before she could think of her next move she heard voices in the hall. Carl, with his handsome good looks, his glossy black hair and startling blue eyes, walked in. His full lips pulled back into his familiar movie star smile, showing white-white teeth, when he saw Joleen. "There you are." He raked his gaze across her, and the smile fell fractionally. "What the hell are you wearing?"

She looked down at her once-formal dress, now dotted with mud, straw and hay pollen. She could see her mussed hair and the circles under her eyes mirrored in Carl's expression.

"I've been up all night. Trouble had colic."

"Trouble?" Had that deep baritone voice always sounded so fake?

"One of Jake's horses."

Carl looked at his mother, who had come in with him. "I might have known Jake would have something to do with this." He put his smile back on and walked over to Joleen. "Never mind, sweetheart, this actually works out rather well." He turned to Virginia. "Wouldn't you say?"

"Indeed," was the chilly reply.

They both turned to look at Joleen. Suddenly she felt like a Thanksgiving turkey on a platter. "What's going on?"

"Mother is going to help you revamp your image."

"*Revamp* my image?" she echoed dumbly. "I didn't know my image needed revamping."

The door banged open behind her and she knew, without looking, that Jake had come in. She could feel his eyes on her back.

Carl's eyes shifted to a spot behind her. "Hello, Jake," he said with a quick nod.

"Carl," came the reply, in a voice she'd heard so much in her head it was as familiar as her own.

Carl returned his attention to Joleen. "As I was

saying, Mother will take you out and help you pick a new wardrobe *and* she's made an appointment for you to have your hair done at her favorite salon.''

"Have my hair done?" She crossed her arms in front of her. "What, exactly, do I need to have done to my hair?"

"Just a little," he touched his own hair, thinking, "coloring."

"Coloring?"

He lowered his brow. "Joleen, you needn't repeat everything I say." His expression lightened. "I'm merely talking about making your hair color a little darker, just a little more dignified. Less, how do I put this, *working class.*"

Joleen fumed. She *had* to keep focused on the point. She had to disentangle herself from Carl, and as soon as she did, this sort of insult wouldn't touch her. "Carl, we need to talk. Privately."

He looked at his watch. "I'm short on time at the moment, how about after dinner?"

She couldn't wait any longer. "No, I really think we'd better do it now."

He took his briefcase off the table. "I'm sure it can wait."

"Carl, it *can't* wait!"

He stopped. "All right." He set the case down. "What is it?"

She glanced at his mother and thought of Jake behind her. "Not here."

"If you all will excuse me, I have something to do," Jake said. He went to Virginia and tried to take her by the arm. "Mother, don't you have something else to do?"

"I'm visiting with my son, whom I haven't seen in days."

"Yes, you can talk in front of Mother, Joleen. It's fine."

Jake met her eyes, and she noticed he made a valiant effort to move Virginia again. "I need you to show me something upstairs, Mother."

"It can wait." She settled her chilly gaze on Joleen.

"Come on, Joleen," Carl prodded. "I need to get out of here."

She took a deep, steadying breath. "So do I."

"Hmm?" Carl asked absently.

"I need to get out of here. I need to go."

He met her eyes. "Where do you need to go?"

"Home."

"What?" Carl looked shocked. Behind him, his mother looked hopeful, and Jake looked...interested. No big, comical emotions there.

Joleen looked from one face to the next, settling on Carl. "I'm sorry, Carl, but I can't marry you."

"Hmm. What brought this on?" He turned pointedly to Jake.

"Nothing brought it on. It's just not right. When something's not right there's no point in pushing it." She shrugged. "I couldn't do you any good, anyway. I'm always tripping over myself and saying the wrong thing."

Carl clicked his tongue against his teeth and moved toward Joleen, glancing once again at his watch. "You just need a little persuasion. Give me a couple of hours and I'll come back and take you to that hairdresser's personally. We can talk in the car on the way."

"No, Carl, that's the whole point. I don't want to change my hair, I don't want to change the way I talk, I don't want to change everything about myself to suit your idea of who or what I should be."

"This doesn't sound like the girl I met six months ago."

"It's not. It's not even the girl you talked to six days ago. I was fooling myself, thinking I wasn't good enough and that I *needed* exactly the sort of guidance you were offering. But the truth is, I don't like myself much when I'm playing that role. The old Joleen Wheeler might not be thin or rich or cultured but at least she knew who she was. I want to be her again, Carl. Can't you understand that?"

"No." He picked up his briefcase again and moved toward her. He kissed her lightly on the cheek. "You must be tired. Go get cleaned up and get some rest and we'll talk about all this nonsense later, okay?"

Without waiting for her answer, he breezed out the door.

"You want any more of that hash?" Marge asked.

It was a week later and Joleen was back in the diner. She looked at the greasy plate in front of her and dropped her fork onto it. "No, thanks. I've had enough." She stood up and walked to the counter. "I will have some more coffee, though." She brought the pot back to her table and poured it. "Just like old times, huh?" She gave a dry laugh.

Marge shook her head and took the coffeepot back to the counter. "Don't you start getting blue on me, miss."

Joleen spread the newspaper on the table before her. "I won't, Marge, don't worry."

"What's that yer doin'?"

"Looking for a job."

Marge looked over her shoulder. "Pretty fancy jobs you're looking at—fund-raiser, program coordinator. I'd say someone got her confidence back in spades. But what about school?"

Joleen circled an ad, capped her pen and looked at her friend. "I'm going to take a break from that for now. It's time to start living."

"Don't you need a degree to get a fancy-shmancy job like one of those?"

Joleen shook her head. "Not necessarily. A little talent goes a long way, and I do believe I might have a talent for this sort of thing."

Marge raised her eyebrows but said nothing.

The bells over the door tinkled. Joleen jerked her head in the direction of the door. Hope surged and pounded through her veins, then disappeared as squat little Howie Bloomer, the one and only bus driver in Alvira, waddled in holding a rolled-up newspaper.

"Hello, Miss Joleen," he said with a courteous nod.

"Hey, Howie." Her heart still pounded foolishly. This new habit of looking for Jake every time the door opened was ridiculous. It had only happened once, the day she'd met him, and she knew he wasn't coming back, so why was she torturing herself this way?

She returned her concentration to the newspaper, hardly noticing that the bell over the door jingled again.

Neither did she pay any attention to the steady clop of boots crossing the floor to her table. "I'm looking for a good, old-fashioned barbecue sandwich," a male voice said.

"Well, you've come to the right place," she said vaguely, and waved her hand in the direction of the counter. "Marge will set you up."

He laughed and she stiffened. She knew that laugh. She knew that voice, too, though she hadn't believed it. She looked up, heart pounding anew. Oh, she knew those eyes, that jaw, that mouth... "Jake," she breathed.

He sat down in the booth opposite her, holding her gaze with the warmth of his own. "I wasn't sure what sort of reception I'd get from you."

She nodded mutely.

His smile froze. "I'm still not sure." He hesitated, looking expectant. "Say something."

"I'm really glad to see you." She was gushing and she knew it.

"It's really good to see you, too."

She felt like a teenager talking to the football captain. "How did the board meeting go? The vote?"

He looked pleased. "Mom and pop won."

"I'm so glad." She nodded and scrambled for something innocuous to say, because if she didn't come up with something quick, she'd end up spilling out all the fantasies she'd been having about him since she left. "What are you doing here?" she asked nonchalantly.

"Looking for you."

"Me?" Good Lord, this was exactly how one of those fantasies began.

"Yup." He glanced at the marked newspaper on the table. "See, I need your help."

"With what?"

"Actually, I need you. That is, I need someone with your particular talents to help me out in my business."

She stared at him, hope suspended by confusion. "You're offering me a job?"

"In a manner of speaking, yes." His eyes were alight with humor. "The pay is good, but the hours can be long...sometimes all night long."

Finally she allowed herself hope. "All night, huh?"

He gave a curt nod, but his eyes gleamed with understanding. "Plus I'll need a long-term commitment from you. Can you give me that?"

"Hmm." She tapped her pen against her chin and regarded him thoughtfully. "How long?"

"A lifetime."

Her breath caught in her throat. Her last shred of caution held back an excited scream. "Go on, I'm listening. What's the catch?"

"Now, I know you didn't like the first offer you got under the Landon heading, but I can assure you this would be a completely different situation." He took a long breath. "Which is not to say that being Mrs. Landon will always be a bed of roses, because it won't. But I promise it will never be a bed of thorns."

All at once a smile touched her lips, and tears sprang to her eyes. "Jake, are you…"

He slipped out of the booth and knelt in front of her on the dingy linoleum floor. "Joleen, will you marry me?"

She clapped her hands to her mouth, then cried, "Yes!"

He looked a little surprised, but stood up and pulled her to her feet. "Are you sure?" he asked, bracing his hands on her shoulders and looking deep into her eyes.

"I am really sure."

"You don't know how glad I am to hear you say that." He reached into his pocket and pulled out a ring box. "It would have been a real drag to have to try and unload this sucker." The ring he took out had a huge glittering diamond on it.

Joleen gasped. "Tell me that's not real."

"Darlin', it's as real as I am." He took her hand gently in his and slid the ring onto her finger. It fit perfectly. He clearly had a gift for sizing that his mother didn't share.

Joleen bit her lower lip and raised her hand to the light. "My Lord, Jake, it's…it's…it's incredible. But we can't afford this right now."

"Why not?"

"The business…we'll just be starting out. I know you aren't part of the Landon oil fortune, but I'm used to being strapped for cash.'' She curled her hand around his neck and ran her fingers through his hair. ''But being strapped with you is going to be a lot better than being strapped alone. Of course, I'm sure this horse breeding will take off, especially with Trouble back on her feet.'' She gave him a reassuring smile. ''Someday we'll look back together on these early days of struggle and feel all the richer for it.''

He smiled broadly. ''That's a real nice thought.'' He pulled her close and, with his mouth just centimeters from hers, added, ''It's that spirit of facing things and overcoming them that made me fall in love with you.''

She leaned her head back. ''Say it again.''

He bent down and kissed the hollow of her throat. ''I love you.''

She lifted her head and said dreamily, ''I love you, too.''

He closed his mouth over hers and held it for a lingering kiss. When he pulled back he said, ''But there's something serious I have to discuss with you.''

Dread dropped like a rock in her stomach. ''What is it? Is it bad? Is it *really* bad?''

''Now, I don't know. How disappointed would you be if we didn't get to go through all that struggling and starving business?''

She frowned. ''What do you mean?''

''I mean I'd do anything for you, and if you want to eat beans for dinner for the next ten years we can, but, you know, it's not,'' he shrugged, ''necessary. I mean, I said I wasn't in the family business, but I didn't say I was a pauper.''

She stepped back and put her hands on her hips. ''Be blunt. Are you telling me you're rich?''

He colored faintly. ''Well, that would depend on your definition of rich.''

She looked at the ring on her finger, then waved it in front of him. ''Rich enough to afford this without sacrifice?''

''Oh, yeah.'' His response was so easy, so casual, that she almost thought she'd heard wrong. She'd assumed, all this time, that he was the stereotypical black sheep of the family, who ran off to live in a commune rather than live the life of ease he'd been brought up in. All at once she realized what she should have heard him saying all the time: it wasn't the wealth he had a problem with, it was the means.

Of *course* a guy like that would have gone out and made his *own* fortune.

She shook her head. ''Jake Landon, there is just so much to learn about you, I don't even know where to begin.''

He took her hand and brought it to his lips. ''At least you have the time now.'' He kissed her hand, then pressed it close to his heart. ''A lifetime.''

* * * * *

Return to the Towers!

In March
New York Times bestselling author

NORA ROBERTS

brings us to the Calhouns' fabulous
Maine coast mansion and reveals the
tragic secrets hidden there for generations.

For all his degrees, Professor Max Quartermain has a
lot to learn about love—and luscious Lilah Calhoun is
just the woman to teach him. Ex-cop Holt Bradford is
as prickly as a thornbush—until Suzanna Calhoun's
special touch makes love blossom in his heart.
And all of them are caught in the race to solve
the generations-old mystery of a priceless
lost necklace...and a timeless love.

Lilah and Suzanna
THE
Calhoun Women

**A special 2-in-1 edition containing
FOR THE LOVE OF LILAH and
SUZANNA'S SURRENDER**

Available at your favorite retail outlet.

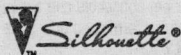

Silhouette®

CWVOL2

Take 4 bestselling love stories FREE

a FREE surprise gift!

ATTENTION ALL
SANDRA STEFFEN
FANS!

Silhouette Books proudly presents four brand-new titles by award-winning author Sandra Steffen for your reading pleasure.

Look for these upcoming titles in 1998:

In February
MARRIAGE BY CONTRACT (*36 Hours* Book #8)
Sandra Steffen's contribution to Silhouette's latest continuity series is a marriage-of-convenience story you won't forget.

In April
NICK'S LONG-AWAITED HONEYMOON
(SR#1290, 4/98)
The popular *Bachelor Gulch* series continues with a tale of reunited lovers.

In July
THE BOUNTY HUNTER'S BRIDE (SR#1306, 7/98)
This contribution to Silhouette's newest promotion, *Virgin Brides,* is a story of a shotgun marriage that leads to the most romantic kind of love.

And coming your way in December from Silhouette Romance, *Bachelor Gulch's* most famous bachelorette, Louetta, finally gets the man of her dreams!

Don't miss any of these delightful stories...
Only from Silhouette Books.

Available at your favorite retail outlet.

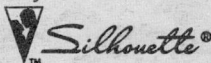

Silhouette®

Look us up on-line at: http://www.romance.net   SRSSTITLES

MONTANA Mavericks™

RETURN TO WHITEHORN

Silhouette's beloved **MONTANA MAVERICKS** returns with brand-new stories from your favorite authors! Welcome back to Whitehorn, Montana—a place where rich tales of passion and adventure are unfolding under the Big Sky. The new generation of Mavericks will leave you breathless!

Coming from Silhouette Special Edition®:

February 98: LETTER TO A LONESOME COWBOY by Jackie Merritt

March 98: WIFE MOST WANTED by Joan Elliott Pickart

May 98: A FATHER'S VOW by Myrna Temte

June 98: A HERO'S HOMECOMING by Laurie Paige

And don't miss these two very special additions to the Montana Mavericks saga:

MONTANA MAVERICKS WEDDINGS
by Diana Palmer, Ann Major and Susan Mallery
Short story collection available April 98

WILD WEST WIFE by Susan Mallery
Harlequin Historicals available July 98

Round up these great new stories
at your favorite retail outlet.

**ALICIA
SCOTT**

Continues the
twelve-book series—
36 Hours—in March 1998
with Book Nine

PARTNERS IN CRIME

The storm was over, and Detective Jack Stryker finally had a
prime suspect in Grand Springs' high-profile murder case. But
beautiful Josie Reynolds wasn't about to admit to the crime—
nor did Jack want her to. He believed in her innocence, and he
teamed up with the alluring suspect to prove it. But was he
playing it by the book—or merely blinded by love?

For Jack and Josie and *all* the residents of Grand Springs,
Colorado, the storm-induced blackout was just the beginning of
36 Hours that changed *everything!* You won't want to miss a
single book.

Available at your favorite retail outlet.

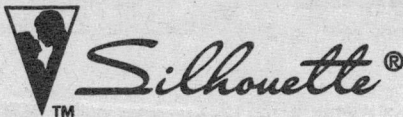

Silhouette®

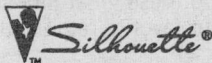

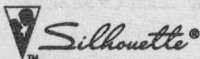